CHARMED BY THE FOX'S HEART

ARIA WINTER

JADE WALTZ

Purple Fall Publishing

Published in the United States by Purple Fall Publishing. Purple Fall Publishing and the Purple Fall Publishing Logos are trademarks and/or registered trademarks of Purple Fall Publishing LLC.-purplefallpublishing.com

Publisher's Cataloging-in-Publication data

Names: Winter, Aria, author. | Waltz, Jade, author.

Title: Charmed by the fox's heart / Aria Winter & Jade Waltz.

Series: Cosmic Guardians

Description: Purple Fall Publishing, 2021.

Identifiers: ISBN:

978-1-64253-207-4 (pbk)

978-1-64253-407-8 (ebook)

978-1-64253-403-0 (audio)

Subjects: LCSH Reincarnation--Fiction. | Magic--Fiction. | Man-woman relationships--Fiction. | Love stories. | Paranormal fiction. | Paranormal romance stories. | Science fiction. | BISAC FICTION / Romance / Paranormal | FICTION / Romance / Science Fiction

Classification: PS3623 .I6675 C53 2021 | DDC 813.6--dc23

Dedication

To my husband: Thank you for all your love and support. You are not just my husband, you are my best friend and my rock. I love you more than anything.

-Aria Winter

To My Husband,
Thank you for being my support and rock during this writing journey. I love you!

-Jade Waltz

CHAPTER 1

KYRA

I dream of fire and ruin... death and destruction. A man with teal eyes holds me in his arms as I lay dying. I do not know who he is. I only know his gaze holds such intense sadness, it tears at my heart. Ash falls around us like snow as dark clouds roll overhead. I touch his face and brush away the tears that fall from his lashes as I offer him my forgiveness.

"It was not you," I whisper. "I know it was not you."

I wake with a start and jerk up in bed. The fog of my nightmares retreats like tides from the shore. I clutch my chest, drawing in several deep breaths as I attempt to calm my rapidly beating heart. When I look down at my palms, I half expect to see blood on my skin, but there is nothing.

It was only a nightmare.

Throwing my legs over the side of the bed, I place my head in my hands. Roughly running my fingers through my hair, I sigh heavily in frustration. I don't understand why I keep having this horrible dream. What does it mean?

I've always had an overactive imagination. That's part of the reason I decided to pursue my dream of writing. At first, I thought this nightmare was a new story percolating in my head like so many others have done before. But now I'm beginning to wonder. This feels real, somehow—more like a memory than something I imagined.

Some nights it's so bad, I actually feel as if there is a wound in my side. I wake up panicked and immediately check my torso, expecting to find bleeding, but there is nothing there. I went to a therapist, and they said it's my mind's way of trying to resolve some issue or other, but I don't believe it. Something happened to me—some kind of deep-rooted trauma—to make me relive this same dream almost every single night. I just have to figure out what it is.

Maybe it has something to do with the death of my mother and sister. I went to a seer shortly after they died. She told me something strange about my recurring dreams. She said the man that holds me is my soulmate—the one I'm destined to find. But I'm not entirely sure I believe in such things.

However, it would certainly make a compelling story for one of my books.

A low rumble sounds as the building begins to shake, ripping me from my thoughts. I brace myself on the edge of the bed, waiting for it to stop. It's over in less than a minute and I'm glad. I hate earthquakes.

It seems like there have been more and more lately over the past few months here in Seattle. I guess we're lucky that scientists figured out how to suppress the bigger ones that used to plague this part of the world less than one hundred years ago. But still... I'm always a little scared when they happen anyway.

I glance up at my clock and immediately hit the panic button when I realize I've overslept.

Somehow, it only takes me fifteen minutes to shower, brush my teeth, and dress. I take a quick glance in the hallway mirror to check that I look okay. My long, blond hair is twisted up in a clip on the back of my head, the best I could do on short notice.

It's my no-nonsense look for the day. Despite how tired I am, you'd never know it. My blue eyes don't have even the slightest hint of redness or puffiness around my lids after a shower and a quick cup of coffee. I didn't have time for makeup, so the several small freckles that cover the bridge of my nose and cheeks are visible, but I don't care. I put a dab of pink lip gloss on, satisfied I now look presentable, and that's all that matters.

I cringe when my bag slams into the wall as I spin to lock the door behind me. A quick glance in my satchel reassures me my precious laptop hasn't broken. Thank goodness.

I'm supposed to meet my best friend for coffee, and I cannot be late. Claire runs on a tight schedule; she plans everything out at least two weeks in advance. Whereas I'm more of a spur-of-the-moment person. I always have been. That's why I'm surprised we've been friends as long as we have, but I suppose it's because we complement each other in that way.

I don't want to disappoint her by arriving late for our meet up like I did last week. She's the closest thing I have to a sister. Besides, if I show up late, she'll have extra time to flirt with Aris—my favorite barista and sort-of crush for the past few months since he started working there. Apparently, he caught her eye last time we met at the coffee house.

Claire is gorgeous. Every time we go somewhere together, I feel like a mere mortal standing next to her goddess-like beauty. Normally, I wouldn't care who she flirts with, but this guy is different.

With chestnut hair that falls just below his brow line and emerald eyes, he's so handsome and charismatic with his signature crooked smile, I have trouble finding words sometimes when I'm around him. But he's not just my crush, he's kind of a friend at this point. I spend so much time at the coffee house, writing during the day, we've gotten to know each other a bit.

To be honest, I'm kind of hoping maybe we can be more than just friends, but I'm still too nervous to make any sort of move. And Claire goes through boyfriends rather quickly. She loses interest pretty much around the two-week mark and I… don't like the idea of that happening between her and Aris.

As I race down the hallway, I notice the lift doors closing up ahead. "Wait!" I call out, hoping whoever is inside will hear me. If they don't, that's yet another delay I cannot afford while I wait for the next one.

A hand appears on the door, stopping it before it fully closes. I reach them just as they reopen, and when I step inside, I realize the hand is attached to a very handsome man. I've seen him a few times before, but we've never spoken. He must live on a floor above me somewhere.

"Thanks." I smile as I step into the lift.

"No problem." He gives me a shy grin.

I take a moment to study him. He has short-cropped, stark white hair, not at all the natural white of someone with age. No, this guy looks to be maybe my age or just a bit older, so somewhere between twenty-four and twenty-five, I would think. He's tall with broad shoulders and solidly built of lean muscle that defines his arms and legs. His square jaw could cut glass, and I could lose myself in his violet eyes for days. His cheeks flush as his gaze holds mine.

Heat creeps up my neck to my face, and I quickly avert my eyes. I hate that I blush so easily. It's the bane of my existence.

"You live on four?" he asks.

"Yeah." Nervous, I tuck a stray tendril of hair behind my ear. "What floor do you live on?"

"The fifth. I'm in 502. I just moved in a few weeks ago."

"You're directly above me," I reply. "I live in 402. My name's Kyra." The moment the words leave my mouth, I fight the urge to facepalm myself. What if he's some kind of stalker? I've just told him my exact apartment number.

A handsome grin curves his lips. "I'm Davin. So, you're the one who plays all that Beethoven that keeps me up all night."

My mouth drifts open. Beethoven is my go-to when I need inspiration for my books. Sometimes, I keep it playing in the background while I'm writing.

"You can hear that?"

He nods. "Who couldn't?"

My mouth drifts open in horror as I realize I'm one of those loud and obnoxious neighbors, and I didn't even know it. "Oh my gosh. I am so sorry. I didn't think I had it on that loud."

"It's no problem," he says quickly. "It helps me to relax sometimes when I'm stressed."

"Me, too."

He smiles. "Would you like to maybe get a cup of coffee sometime?"

My cheeks flush with warmth. "Sure."

His smile grows even brighter. "Great."

As soon as the lift reaches the first floor, he gestures for me to step out first, then follows behind me.

"Well, it was nice meeting you," he says. "I'm looking

forward to our coffee. Let me know when would be a good time for you."

"All right," I reply a bit awkwardly, then turn to walk toward the café. I'm only ten steps away when I glance over my shoulder and notice him still watching me. He gives me a nervous grin, then shakes his head softly as if caught before he turns away and starts down the street.

A smile tugs at my lips. I'm looking forward to that cup of coffee with him. As I walk along the sidewalk, weaving through the throng of people, I wonder if I should wait a few days before I ask him out.

Doubt begins to creep in. What if I seemed too eager to go out with him, and now he's got the wrong impression? What if we go on a date and he finds out I'm a romance writer? Then, after he reads all those steamy scenes, what if he expects I'll just fall into his arms at the end of the night or something like that? All sorts of troubling scenarios begin to play out in my mind. I'm so in my head when I reach the café, I almost miss Claire as she raises a hand to catch my attention.

"Kyra!" she calls out. "I'm over here. I already got a table."

I roll my eyes. Of course, she picked the table closest to the counter. She has a thing for my barista crush—Aris—just like I do. I dart a quick glance at the bar and notice, "Mr. Dreamy," as she calls him, is not here today. Instead, there is someone new working the register. His back is turned, so I can't really see him clearly, but from her grin it's easy to see he's already caught her eye.

When I reach the table, she gestures to the counter. "Your guy's not here today."

My mouth drifts open. I've never told her I have a crush on Aris. Is it that obvious though? "How did you know?"

She shrugs as a sly smirk quirks her lips. "I'm your best

friend. How could I not? Besides, why do you think I left him alone?"

I smile. "Thanks, Claire."

We leave a placeholder at the table, then walk to the counter to stand in the queue. It doesn't take long to reach the front, and when we do, my mouth drifts open as soon as the new guy turns to face us.

A handsome grin curves his lips. "What would you like?"

My gaze travels over his straight, white hair, hanging down just enough he has to brush it back from his gorgeous teal eyes. My jaw drops when I recognize them as the same eyes I see every night in my dreams. The seer's words repeat in my mind. She told me that man was my destined soulmate.

I stare at up him in astonishment. He looks like he's around twenty-five or so. He's tall and lean but in a muscular way, with broad shoulders, an aristocratic nose, cheeks, and brow and a square jaw that could cut glass.

In the corner of my vision, I notice Claire flash her best smile at him and jealousy instantly flares to life inside me.

I'm relieved, however, when I notice that he seems surprisingly immune to her charms. That's strange. No man can resist Claire's charismatic personality. At least, not until now. When he smiles and asks me again for my order, his teal eyes lock on mine, and I've suddenly forgotten how to speak.

"You're new," the words escape my lips before I even realize I've said them aloud.

He gives me a handsome grin. "My name is Cael. What's yours?"

I've never been speechless before over a guy. But he's so gorgeous I'm completely mesmerized as he stares down at me. It takes me a moment to even remember how to form words. Finally, I reply, "Kyra."

"Well, Kyra." He grins. "What would you like?" He gestures to the menu behind him. "Anything you want, it's on the house."

I blink up at him. "Won't your boss get angry if you start giving stuff away for free?"

"Well, you happen to be in luck because—" His expression falls as he darts a glance over my shoulders. "Hold on a moment. I'll be right back."

Before I can say anything, he jumps over the counter and rushes to the door. Pushing it open, I watch in horror as he races out into traffic.

Vehicles honk and slam on their breaks, barely avoiding hitting him as he rushes to the middle of the busy road.

"What's he doing?" Claire's voice rings out behind me. "He's going to get killed!"

"That guy's crazy!" someone calls out.

I gasp as he barely misses being hit as he makes his way to a small, orange ball of fluff. It's a cat. Its green eyes are wide with terror as it stands frozen in the middle of the road. Cael scoops it up in his arms and somehow manages to dart back through traffic as he returns to the café. Everyone watches, gaping as he pulls the door open to come back inside.

He walks up to me and I stare at him in shock. "You could have been killed!"

He gives me a beaming smile as he cradles the orange cat to his chest, gently stroking its fur. It leans into his touch and starts to purr. "I couldn't let this poor little thing get run over, now could I?"

I've always been an animal lover, and seeing this handsome man lovingly petting this cat, makes my heart melt.

"It's all right," he whispers soothingly. "You're safe now, little one."

I think I'm in love.

He looks back at me. "Could you please watch her for a

bit?" He holds out the cat. "I have to take orders, and I,"—he darts a glance around the room—"don't think some of the customers would be too happy if I took her behind the counter with me."

"N—no problem," I stumble over my words as he hands the cat to me. Instead of being nervous about the exchange, the cat appears relaxed as he transfers her to my arms.

Movement behind Cael catches my eye and I smile when Aris leans over his shoulder and winks at me. "Hey, Kyra." His eyes sweep briefly to Claire and he nods before returning his attention right back to me. "It's good to see you again."

Aris is devastatingly handsome, and he knows it. With his short, chestnut hair and emerald eyes, he's gorgeous—tall, lean, muscular, and confident. He's always flirting with me, but I force myself to brush it off because I don't know if he's serious or if it's just his personality. I've seen several women flirt with him in return, and he seems to enjoy all the attention. I just... I can't tell if he's actually interested in me, so I play it safe with him, trying not to get my hopes up too much.

"I thought you weren't here today." I smile back at him.

"Someone called in, so I'm working mostly in the back. But my friend,"—he claps a hand on Cael's shoulder—"Cael came to the rescue." He narrows his eyes at him. "Speaking of rescue... Why are you always so impulsive? You could have died just now."

"You're being dramatic." Cael rolls his eyes. "And, I'm not impulsive."

Aris purses his lips. "Yes, you are."

"You expected me to just watch a cat get run over?" He gestures exaggeratively to the cat in my arms. "I couldn't stand by and do nothing."

Aris reaches across the counter and gently pats its head,

then scratches under its chin. "You're lucky my best friend is so reckless," he coos. "Yes, you are."

Cael sighs heavily in mock irritation, but I notice the faint smile that tugs at his lips as he looks to Aris.

I study Cael a moment. Why does he look exactly like the man in my recurring dreams? I mean... it's too strange to be just a coincidence. Isn't it?

The cat begins purring like crazy in my arms as Aris continues to lavish attention on her.

Cael looks to the orange ball of fur, and then darts a glance toward the kitchen. "Wait a minute." He turns and races into the back, appearing a moment later with a small bowl of milk. "You can give this to her." He hands it to me and gestures to the cat. "I'll get your drink and take it to your table when it's ready. What would you like me to make for you?"

Aris looks to Cael. "Kyra likes the vanilla latte with an extra shot to start off the day." He winks at me. "Unless you've decided to try something new?"

Cael's eyes meet mine, and I'm completely flustered, so I quickly shake my head.

"No, the regular will do just fine this morning."

Aris elbows Cael. "That's her first drink of the day. I'll let you know the rest later on."

His brow furrows in confusion. "The... rest?"

"She's a regular here," Aris explains. "She's a writer, and she spends most of her time writing here in the café."

Cael's eyes practically light up. "Then, be sure to let me know what you want, and I'll get it ready for you. After all," his gaze darts to the cat, "we're practically sharing custody now. It's the least I can do."

I laugh. A warm flush creeps across my cheeks as his gaze holds mine. "Thank you."

"Anything for the adoptive mother of my cat," he teases.

"*Your* cat?" I arch a brow. "What if *I* want to keep her?"

He laughs. "We'll work out the custody arrangement later."

We haven't even made it all the way back to our table when Claire grabs my arm and pulls me close to her and whispers in my ear.

"Oh my gosh, I think that new guy has a thing for you." She's practically beaming. "And he's such a knight in shining armor. I can't believe he risked his life like that."

I glance down at the orange, purring ball of fur in my arms. The cat lifts its head, green eyes locking on mine as if listening in on our conversation. I gently stroke her fur.

"That brave man saved you, didn't he?" I coo to her. "Yes, he did."

Remembering Claire's statement, I dart a glance over my shoulder and find Cael's eyes on me. He smiles, then turns to the next customer, running his hands through his silken, white hair to smooth it back. Could someone that gorgeous really be into me? This is the second hot guy who has flirted with me today.

I look back at Claire. "What makes you say that?"

"The way he was staring at you and flirting with you." She huffs and then rolls her eyes. "Really, Kyra, you couldn't tell?"

I shrug. "Well, it's just weird, I guess. He's the second guy today who seemed interested and,"—I look down at myself, remembering how quickly I dressed and got ready to come here—"I'm not even made up."

"You don't have to be made up, Kyra. You're beautiful."

I open my mouth to protest I look rather drab today, but she starts speaking again.

"Trust me. It's natural for you. I'm a bit jealous, to be honest. I mean,"—she gestures to herself—"this magnificence you see before you doesn't just happen on its own. It takes a great deal of work each morning to maintain."

I purse my lips. "Sure, it does, Claire," I say sarcastically.

"All right." She tips up her chin and flips her hair back dramatically. "You've got me. I know I'm naturally gorgeous. But so are you. I don't know why you doubt it."

"I guess I just feel plain sometimes, you know?" I shrug, ready to move on from the conversation. Even as I ask this question, I know she has no idea what I'm talking about. Claire is so charismatic, people seem to be naturally drawn in by her energy. That's why she's so good at her job. She completely captivates her audience each afternoon and evening on the local news.

We talk for a while before she has to leave. As soon as she's gone, I look to my cat companion, wondering what to do. I could take her home, but I don't have any supplies. Besides, wouldn't she be lonely if I just left her there?

Speaking of, she's awfully calm, as far as cats go. She isn't on a leash, but so far, she's stayed right by my side, curled up on the bench next to me and contentedly purring away, her small bowl of milk nearby for when she gets hungry.

Satisfied she's happy, I take out my computer and order some supplies for her to be delivered to my apartment. I can hardly wait to show her new home to her. I know this was supposed to be temporary, but I'm definitely keeping her. I don't know where she came from or how she ended up in the middle of the street, but when she gets up and snuggles against me, flipping onto her back, I'm completely in love with my new companion.

I give her some belly rubs as I think on a new plot for my story. As a writer, I'm constantly working, even when it seems I'm not. For almost the entire time Claire was talking to me, I was already imagining a new romance about a brave barista who rescues a cat and then falls in love with his regular customer.

The thing is, I like Aris *and* Cael, so I'm going to have to make my character a mixture of them both I suppose.

As if my very thoughts have summoned him, Cael appears at my table. Startled, my eyes snap up to meet his.

"I brought you your mid-morning drink." He carefully arranges it next to my laptop. "And one for our cat." I laugh as he refers to her as "ours." He replaces her bowl of milk with a fresh one and she lifts her head to blink up at him before going to it.

"Thanks." I glance down at the cat-shaped foam on my drink and smile. Gently, I swirl the cup, trying to see how dark the coffee is below the design. "What is this?"

"It's something I just whipped up."

I lift it to my mouth to take a small sip. I'm surprised at the decadent dark chocolate flavor that rolls across my tongue with just a hint of raspberry. "Mmmm, this is delicious."

Over his shoulder, I see Aris's defeated look as Cael asks me what I think. "You like it?"

"It's great. What do you call it?"

Cael gives me a handsome grin. "It's a dark chocolate, raspberry cocoa."

My mouth drifts open. I'm not sure how I feel about it now. "No caffeine?" I ask, unable to mask my disappointment.

He winks. "I put a shot in there for you."

"Thanks." I lift the cup to him. "I think this is my new favorite."

He eyes the cat. "So how should we work out the shared custody?"

I reach down and run my fingers over her long soft fur, and she purrs even louder. I tip my head up slightly as I tease him. "There won't be any shared custody. I'm going to keep her all to myself."

"Well, I guess you'll have to bring her to visit me here then." He chuckles. "And let me know when her soccer games are so I can at least show up for those."

I grin. "I'll be sure to do that." I meet his gaze evenly. "That was really brave what you did back there to save her."

"I couldn't allow a helpless creature to be injured while I stood there and watched. No one else was trying to help her, and I didn't want to watch her get run over."

I nod because I know if I had seen her first, I probably would've done the same as well.

"Have you thought of a name?"

"Not yet." I glance down at the cat in my lap as I scratch her chin, smiling as she purrs. "But I have a feeling it will come to me."

Across the room, Aris narrows his eyes at Cael as he calls out to him. "There's a line forming back here, you know."

Cael smiles at me again, then leans in just a bit and whispers. "If you like that drink, I think I have another one you'll like next."

I blink up at him, my face flushing with warmth as his teal gaze holds mine. "Thanks," I somehow manage.

He winks, and I'm completely captivated as a faint smile tugs at his gorgeous full lips. "I'll be back soon."

Just like that, I'm inspired to write even more. The words practically flow from my fingertips as I furiously type on my keyboard. My hero is a handsome barista by day and a crime fighter by night. He falls in love with the writer, who spends her days at the café with her loyal cat companion, drinking coffee as she works on her award-winning novel.

"What are you working on?" a male voice practically purrs in my ear.

Slightly startled, I turn and find Cael staring down at me, his eyes sparkling with amusement as he places another cup next to my laptop. I glance at the clock, shocked that two hours have already gone by while I was typing. Instead of answering, I ask, "What's this one?" I bring the warm mug to my nose and breathe in the delicious scent. It smells amazing.

"Cinnamon, chocolate, peppermint latte." He winks. "If you don't like it, I can try something else."

Aris clears his throat and calls out to Cael from the counter, "Could you please leave my favorite customer alone?"

Cael arches a brow. "She's not just *your* customer, you know. She's mine, too."

Aris crosses his arms. "Is that so?"

"Yeah," Cael laughs. "Fifty-fifty, remember?"

My brow furrows as I look between the two of them. "Wait a minute… you're the owners?"

Aris tips his chin up with pride. "The owner was selling, so Cael and I decided to buy it. The paperwork just went through yesterday."

"Wow, congratulations!"

My gaze flicks back up to Cael. I guess that means I'll be seeing more of him around here, and to be honest, I like that idea.

"Thank you." Cael's eyes are full of mischief as he leans over to catch a glimpse of my screen. He flicks his gaze back to mine. "You never told me what you're working on."

Slightly flustered, I open my mouth to reply but then stop, unsure of what to tell him. I'm not sure I really want him to know what I write. I know I could easily make something up, but it's never a good idea to start a relationship—friendship or otherwise—with deception. So, I draw in a deep breath and decide to tell him the truth.

"It's a romance novel." I brace myself for the inevitable teasing I've received in the past from others I've told.

Instead, he gives me a curious look. "What's it about?"

My cheeks heat with embarrassment. I'm certainly not going to tell him about my hero barista. So instead, I shrug. "You know… typical love story. Guy meets girl, and they fall in love."

He nods. "I'd like to read it when you're done."

"You would?"

"Yeah." He grins as he leans in. His warm, minty breath fans across my ear as he whispers, "I'm a sucker for romance."

"Hey!" Aris snaps. "Would you stop pestering Kyra? Get back here and help me."

Cael laughs and waves him off. "I'll be right there." He leans down and pets the cat. She rolls over, stretching out so he can run his hand over her belly before he gently scratches beneath her chin.

I smile as I watch him. This guy is the whole package. As he makes his way back to the counter, I allow my gaze to travel over his lean, muscular form. Like a marble statue of masculine perfection, this guy is almost too perfect to be real. With a dreamy sigh, I sit back in my chair and then turn my attention back to my writing. I'm completely inspired to write romance today, especially after meeting Cael.

CHAPTER 2

CAEL

As I work behind the counter, it's hard to keep my gaze from drifting to Kyra. There's something about her that draws me in, and it's hard to focus on anything else. I've heard of love at first sight, but never really believed in it… until now.

I study her a moment. Her blond hair has almost completely fallen out of her clip, cascading down her shoulders in long, silken waves. I sigh as I think on her luminous blue eyes, her dazzling smile, and the warm flush of her face as she stared up at me, accentuating the slight dusting of freckles across her cheeks and the bridge of her nose.

With her eyes glued to her computer, she steadily types away while sipping on the drinks I've made for her. I don't know how Aris operates, but as far as I'm concerned, I'll give her all her drinks for free to encourage her to come in here every day.

Now, I just have to walk the fine line between crazy guy she just met that wants to marry her already and cool guy who wants to ask her out on a casual date—which will actually be anything but casual—to get the ball rolling on this relationship.

One of my foster moms—actually, she was more like a foster grandma due to her age—told me that the first time she saw her husband, she knew he was the man she was going to marry. I remember thinking that story was so crazy, but now as I glance back at Kyra, I get it.

Aris always says I'm impulsive, and maybe I am. But right now, I don't care. There's just something about Kyra that feels right.

A hand claps me on the shoulder. I look back at Aris, and he gives me a pointed look.

"Kitchen. Now."

I look over at Tara, who's mostly been making the orders. I ask her to watch the register, and she agrees as I head into the back kitchen with Aris.

As soon as I step through the doors, he spins to face me, a thunderous look on his face. He lifts his hand, pointing a finger at me with mock authority.

"Don't even think about it," he snaps.

I blink at him, shocked by his sharp words and expression.

"Think about what?"

"Kyra. *That's* what," he hisses, gesturing in the direction she is sitting just beyond the door. "She's my best customer."

"And?" I ask incredulously.

"I don't want you flirting with her."

"*You* flirt with her," I protest. "So, how is that fair?"

"No, I don't."

"Yes," I state firmly, "you do. I watched it go down."

His stony expression softens, and he rolls his eyes.

"All right, fine, I do, but that's different."

"How is that different?"

"It just is, all right?"

I arch a brow. He must really be into her because it's not like him to tell me who I can or cannot flirt with. I'm about to speak, but Tara's voice draws our attention.

"Uh, guys?" she calls through the door, and our heads both snap toward her. "The lunch crowd is here. We're starting to get a line."

I dart a glance at Aris, wordlessly promising to discuss this more later, and we head back to the front to take care of our customers.

My eyes sweep back to Kyra's table to find her staring directly at me. A pink bloom spreads across her cheeks and the bridge of her nose the moment her gaze meets mine, and she quickly looks back down at her computer. I'm fairly certain she's attracted to me, but... her face reddened when she talked to Aris earlier too. Maybe she's just shy.

I look back at Aris, working on heating another batch of pastries. We met in college and have been friends for the past five years. Owning and operating a café has always been our dream, and now that we finally have it, we're already at a crossroads concerning a customer.

Correction—the woman of my dreams.

With a heavy sigh, I force myself to focus. After a while, the line begins to die down as the lunch hour ends. So far, it's been a great day for business, but as I dart a glance first at Kyra and then to my friend... a terrible day for our friendship.

I mix up another drink for Kyra and take it to her table. It's almost like I can feel Aris's eyes on my back as I make my way toward her. Despite my resolve not to be nosy, I can't help but glance at her screen again as I approach.

My brows go up when I read the steamy snippet from her display, and I wonder if she's the kind of writer who writes what she likes or what she thinks the readers will. Or perhaps she pulls from real-life experience like I've heard many do. If she agrees to go out with me, and things progress, I'm definitely all in for worshipping her like a goddess, like the hero is doing to the heroine in her story right now.

Kyra lifts her gaze to mine and gives me a stunning smile as I present her next drink to her.

She tips the mug toward her with a thoughtful expression. "What's this one?"

I arch a teasing brow. "How about you try it and tell me what you think?"

She laughs as her eyes dance with mirth. "All right."

She brings the cup to her lips and takes a dainty sip, staring up at me from over the rim of the mug. I sit down beside her, petting the cat while she considers my new creation.

The cat stands up and crawls into my lap, purring loudly as I stroke her chin. She's really affectionate. I'm already getting attached, but I don't think Lynx would like her.

Come to think of it, I'm not even sure if a fox and a cat would make good companions to one another. Lynx is definitely not a normal fox, but still...

It's probably for the best that Kyra keeps her. My *familiar* is so dramatic. I'm sure I'd never hear the end of it from Lynx if I came home with a new companion.

As if sensing my thoughts, the cat opens her green eyes and looks up at me. My fingertips warm as I run them over her fur. I glance down and notice the slight tinge of a blue glow following in their wake. My mouth drifts open. I blink, and it disappears, stunning me even more.

This is no ordinary cat. She's a *familiar*, like Lynx. She has to be.

I shake my head as if to clear my thoughts and then look to Kyra. Maybe I'm just tired, and it's causing me to see things. After all, I was a bit concerned about my first day here. This is a joint venture between Aris and me, and there is nothing I want more than for it to be a success.

But then again… maybe there's a reason I feel about her the way that I do. What if Kyra is like me? Maybe that's why I'm drawn to her.

Kyra's eyes light up as she tastes my new creation. She lifts a thoughtful gaze to the ceiling. "Dark chocolate, caramel, and a hint of almond." Her blue eyes search mine. "Am I right?"

This girl is special. I just know it. I feel it deep in my soul. "What do you think? Is it a keeper?"

"Definitely. You should add this one to the regular menu," she adds as she lifts her cup. "I think customers would love it."

"Then, we'll be sure to do that." I wink, already thinking about what else I would like to make for her.

Now, I just need to build up my courage and ask her out.

When she's finished with her drink, she holds her cup out to me. As I take it, my fingers accidentally brush against hers, and a strange warmth moves through me from the contact of her skin. An image flashes in my mind.

I still as I realize it's from my recurring dream—the nightmare that wakes me up in a cold sweat almost every night.

I'm holding a woman. I stare down at her ashen face, her eyelids fluttering open and closed as she fights the death that will claim her.

Tears sting my eyes as I cup her cheek, horrified when I realize too late that my hand is covered in blood as it smears across her face. "Forgive me," I barely manage.

She reaches for me. "It was not you," she whispers. "I know it was not you." Her eyes close, and she goes completely still.

Pain and sadness move through me, consuming everything in

their path, leaving behind nothing but devastation in their wake. I roar my anguish to the sky as I hold her against me.

I draw in a shaking breath as the terrible images slowly retreat from my mind.

Kyra blinks up at me as if stunned. "Did you—" she starts to ask, but her wristband chirps, startling us both. She glances down at the display and then looks back to me. "I—I have to get this. It's my friend, Claire."

Still slightly in shock, I somehow manage to nod. I take her cup and move back behind the counter. My heart taps a frantic beat as I think on what just happened. Numbly, I go to the sink to rinse out the cup. How can this be? Why did her touch make me see the images from my nightmare?

Aris elbows my side, ripping me from my thoughts.

"What's wrong with you?" he smirks. "Tired from a hard day's work already?"

I turn to him with a sober look. "My nightmare, Aris… the same one you have, too. Something just happened."

His expression falls as he scans my face. He knows exactly what I'm talking about. We share this terrible recurring dream but we don't understand why.

"What happened?"

"When I touched her,"—I jerk my chin toward Kyra—"it triggered a… a flash of it for some reason." I meet his eyes evenly. "Has that ever happened to you? With her?"

He clenches his jaw. "I have to be careful, Cael. You know I can't touch people."

Of course, he hasn't ever touched her. I should have remembered. The first time we met, we bumped into each other in the lift at the college. I took his hand to help him back up after he'd fallen, and because he was so stunned, he didn't pull away.

The moment his palm touched mine, a flash of images moved through me. At first, I didn't understand, then he explained. Aris is a touch telepath, able to sense things through the simple act of touch.

The images I saw when I touched him were of my nightmare. Only a few passed through my thoughts at that moment, but when he explained he had the same recurring dreams as I did, we knew it was more than a coincidence. We just didn't understand what it was.

We still don't.

We became friends in our joint search to find answers, but after finding none for the past five years, we sort of gave up, figuring at least we got a friendship out of our shared misery. But now... I look toward Kyra, and Aris does the same.

Perhaps we'll get some answers.

CHAPTER 3

KYRA

Cael's fingers touch mine as he takes my cup. Myriad images flood my mind—most of them from my terrible nightmare that plagues me almost every night.

I pull back my hand as if burned. Drawing in a shaking breath, I meet his teal eyes evenly. "Did you—" I start to ask, but my wristband chirps, startling us both.

I glance down and realize it's a call from my best friend. "I —I have to get this. It's my friend, Claire."

His gaze holds mine a beat before he finally nods and then turns away, heading back behind the counter.

My eyes track his retreating form as I wonder at what just happened between us.

Claire begins talking, but nothing she says is really registering in my mind. My responses are automatic as I do my best to appear normal, despite the fact that I feel anything but normal right now.

After I'm finished talking to Claire, I turn my attention

back to the computer, pretending to study the screen. That has never happened before. Swallowing nervously, I lift my gaze back to Cael.

I don't know if he felt anything like I did, but if so, he didn't say anything. Then again, I said nothing, either.

I look down at the cat and find her green eyes already staring up at me expectantly. I pick her up and cuddle her to my chest. "Are you ready to leave, angel?"

She purrs loudly, and I take that as a hint. It's earlier than my usual time to leave, but after what happened, I doubt I'll get any more words in today. I need to go home, take a nice long bath, and just relax. Maybe I'm just stressed. After all, my last book didn't do as well as I'd hoped and so I'm putting a lot of pressure on myself to get this new one right.

I gather up my belongings, then carefully place my new companion just inside my bag with her head sticking out, so she can see while we walk back to the apartment.

I wave a quick goodbye to Aris and Cael as I start for the door.

"Kyra!" Cael calls out. "Wait!"

I turn back to face him as he walks toward me.

He holds out a to-go cup and gives me a handsome smile. "I thought you might like one for the road."

"Thanks. That's really sweet of you."

His smile grows even wider. "Let me know what you think of this one tomorrow."

I'm mesmerized as I stare deep into his gorgeous eyes. Nervously, I tuck a stray tendril of long blond hair behind my ear. "I—I will," I stumble over my words.

"Great! I'll see you then."

He holds the door open for me like a gentleman as me and my new cat leave the café.

When I reach my apartment building, I step onto the lift. I

press four and then look down at my new best friend, waiting for the doors to close when someone steps on.

I lift my head to see Davin smiling at me.

"Hey, Kyra." His gaze drops to my bag. "I see you picked up a new friend."

"Yeah." I reach down and stroke the top of her head. "I… sort of found her today at the coffee house."

"Great find." He reaches out to pet her and she responds by purring like mad.

"She's my new writing muse," I add proudly.

His brows go up in a thoughtful look. "You're a writer?"

I nod, bracing myself for the inevitable barrage of questions.

"What do you write?"

It occurs to me I could just lie. It's not like he'd know. Normally, that's what I do, especially if a guy asks me. After all, a lot of guys don't respect romance authors, but as my gaze scans Davin, I don't know why, but I don't feel like he'd judge me harshly for this. After all, Cael didn't.

"I write fantasy romance novels."

He smiles. "I love fantasy."

A slow grin curves my mouth. I hadn't expected that kind of reply, but now I know I was right to tell him.

"Do you write under a pen name?"

"No," I reply. "I write under my real name. Kyra Luna."

He looks down at his wristband and types into the display. "Kyra. Luna," he says under his breath. After a moment, he lifts his gaze to me and smiles brightly. "Beneath A Silver Moon," he says. "I'll check it out."

My cheeks heat in embarrassment. That's one of my steamier novels, and I'm not sure it's the one I want him to check out first if he's so determined to read something of mine. I look down at his display and note my other books listed.

"What about starting with that one?" I point to my clean romance novel.

He arches a teasing brow. "But I like the cover on this one better."

I try but fail to suppress a grin. "Fair enough."

He smiles. "I'll let you know what I think after I've read it."

"I… uh… that sounds good," I reply, my voice rising in pitch on the last word as my nerves get the best of me.

"All right." He lifts his wrist as if gesturing to the book still on the display. "I'll read it tonight and… the next time we run into each other, I'll let you know what I thought. Or we could even discuss it if we go for coffee."

"Okay," I smile. "I… look forward to hearing what you think."

The lift stops at my floor and I step off. As I do, I can't help but glance back and notice Davin still watching me. He gives me a nervous smile and a small wave as the doors slide shut.

I look down at my cat and arch a brow. "How is it that I met two handsome guys in the same day?"

She blinks up at me but says nothing. I pet her head and start down the hallway. By the time we reach the apartment, all the supplies I ordered for her are already waiting for me. The boxes are stacked neatly at the door, so I pull them inside as we enter. I set the cat down and give her a good scratch behind her left ear.

"This is your new home, angel," I explain, hoping she will like it. "It's not much, but don't worry. I'll get your food and everything set up so you can be comfy." She turns to me, sitting back on her hind legs as her green eyes stare up at me expectantly.

Now that I think about it, I wonder if she's going to be happy here. My apartment isn't very big, but it's a step up from the studio I was in last year. With one bedroom, a living room, kitchen and bath, it's definitely larger than what I used to have, but I don't know how much space cats need to feel comfortable.

With a heavy sigh I turn to face her. "I'm sorry this is all I have, angel. I'll take you with me every day to the coffee house so you don't get stir crazy in here. How's that sound?"

"My name isn't Angel," she says, and I go completely still. "It's Astra."

My mouth drifts open as I stare down at her. "Did you..." I stop abruptly as I draw in a deep and steadying breath, then release it slowly through my nostrils, attempting to calm myself. Swallowing thickly, I start again.

"Did you just talk?"

"Yes, I did," she replies matter-of-factly. "You are the one I have been searching for. And I am your familiar."

"Me?" I ask, incredulously, still in shock I'm talking to a cat. "What's a familiar?" the question escapes me before I even realize I've spoken it aloud.

She tips her head to the side to regard me. "A familiar is a sort of... companion or spirit animal that is attached to a person. I am here to serve and to guide you."

Am I dreaming? I pinch my hand to try to wake myself up, but nothing happens. I blink down at my new feline companion, stunned.

"You are not dreaming, Kyra. You are the Chosen One. I have been sent by the God of Creation to find you and your guard."

I walk over to the couch and sit down. Placing my head in my hands, I take several deep breaths, attempting to figure out why I'm suddenly having what I'm certain is a mental breakdown.

"You're not crazy, Kyra," Astra says. "You are the Chosen

One, and now that I have found you, we merely need to wait for your guard to arrive."

"My… guard?"

"Yes. The man who saved me."

My jaw drops. "Cael?"

Her lips quirk up in the corners in her best approximation of a smile. "That would be the one." She studies me a moment, tipping her head to the side to regard me. "You sensed something when you touched him, didn't you?"

"Yes, I…" I stop short. How does she know about that? Shaking my head in disbelief, I look down at my hands. "Cael's a barista and you're a cat. I'm talking to a cat… and a cat is talking to me."

A soft huff of air escapes me as I laugh. "Oh my gosh. I've either lost it or I'm still asleep and dreaming."

She moves closer and reaches her paw up to me as if wanting to shake my hand. "Take my paw."

My mouth drifts open but I quickly snap it shut. "Is this… really happening?"

A hint of irritation shifts into her gaze.

Drawing in a deep breath to try to calm myself, I reluctantly do as she asks.

Best case scenario: I'm dreaming. Worst case: I'm insane.

The moment I touch her, images flood my mind like waves crashing against rock. Some of them are from my nightmare with the strange man who looks like Cael, and others are of a life that feels like it's mine, but I know it couldn't possibly be. It's filled with memories of people that are familiar somehow, but I know we've never met.

I relinquish my grip on her paw, and the world begins to spin. I fall back onto the couch as everything tilts around me.

Astra jumps up beside me. "Forgive me," she says. "I know memories of your other life must be overwhelming to receive all at once."

I manage to lift my head. "Memories of my other life? I—I don't understand."

She gives me a pitying look. "They are of your life before… in the Otherworld."

"Otherworld?" I ask, then groan as a headache pounds at my temples.

"I will explain it all as soon as you're well, Kyra," she says softly. "But first, we must find Cael again and speak to him. You will need his help for what is to come."

CHAPTER 4

CAEL

I watch as Kyra leaves the café. Beside me, Aris's eyes track her retreating form as well.

"Something happened before I touched her."

He turns to me, arching an inquisitive brow. "The cat?"

"Yes. I think it's like Lynx and Fin."

"I believe so, too."

I meet his gaze evenly. "What should we do?"

"What can we do?" He shrugs. "We could try to talk to her tomorrow when she comes in."

"*If* she comes in," I mutter, remembering how shocked I was when Lynx first showed up. At first, I'd thought one too many drinks could explain the talking fox, but when I woke up in the morning, completely sober, and he asked what was for breakfast, I hit the panic button. I thought for sure I'd gone crazy. It took me a few days to make peace with it and realize there are more things in this world than we could ever hope to explain with science.

Aris said the same thing happened to him with Fin. To be

honest, I don't know which is worse—a talking fox like Lynx who's always asking for bacon or a peacock like Fin who practically demands to be worshipped like a deity because he thinks he's so beautiful.

As if reading my mind, my friend chuckles.

"I hope the cat's not as insistent as our familiars."

I laugh. "Me, too."

Aris's expression sobers. "She might have the answers we've been looking for. The reason we share the same nightmare."

I meet his gaze evenly. "I hope so."

When I get home, sure enough, Lynx is waiting for me, upset I'm half an hour later than usual.

"What took you so long?" He arches a brow, his bright blue eyes staring at me accusingly. "I'm practically starving."

I roll my eyes. He can be so dramatic sometimes. My gaze travels over his fluffy, white coat which has gotten even "fluffier" lately with all the bacon he's been eating. "You're definitely not going to starve."

His mouth drifts open as he looks down at himself, then back up at me. "If you are implying I've put on some weight, I'd like to remind you that winter is coming. This is just extra fluff and fur. Nothing more." He tilts his head up, indignant.

Truth be told, that extra fluff and fur looks like it weighs a good five pounds more than it did in the summer time.

I laugh as I walk toward the kitchen. "Extra fluff and fur… right," I tease. I turn to him with a sober look. "Actually, I think I've found someone else like us."

He tips his head to the side, curling his fluffy white tail around his feet. "Who?"

"A woman. She was in the café today. I rescued a cat, and she took it home, but when I touched its fur…"

"You sensed magic," he finishes my sentence.

"Yeah, but it's not just that."

"Do tell." He lies on the floor, placing one front paw elegantly atop the other before he turns his full attention to me—extra fluff, tail, and all. He's so cute when he does that, but I can't comment on it. He's sensitive about stuff like that, insisting that when I say such things, he feels more like a pet instead of a companion or familiar.

"When I touched her—the woman—it triggered images of my nightmare. The woman who dies in my arms."

He lowers his gaze, brows pinched together in concern.

"Then, you have finally found her."

My head jerks back in surprise. "Found who?"

"Your queen. The one you guarded in your past life."

"My queen? My past life?" I blink down at him in confusion. "What are you talking about?"

Sitting up, he jerks his chin toward the stool by the counter.

"You may want to sit down."

CHAPTER 5

KYRA

Morning light filters in through the curtains, casting a soft orange glow throughout the room. I sit up in bed, and my head spins a moment before settling. Astra is curled beside me, still sleeping. Without thinking, I reach out to pet her but stop just short when the memories of last night return. Softly, I shake my head. I had to have been dreaming. Cats don't talk.

As if sensing my hesitation, Astra opens her eyes and turns to me.

"Good morning, Kyra," she says, then stretches out her full length on the bed.

I still.

What. The. Hell.

"You're not crazy," she blinks up at me. "I swear."

Her saying that doesn't mean it's not true. I stare at her a moment before delirious laughter bubbles up in my throat.

"This from the cat who I think is talking to me."

She narrows her eyes. "I *am* talking to you." Her expression turns sorrowful. "Do you not remember me at all?"

"What are you talking about?" Yet even as the words leave my mouth, flashes of images rush through my mind. I'm seated on a silver throne dressed in white while Astra sits on the floor beside me.

I reach up and place my palm on my forehead, checking for fever. "What is wrong with me? I don't understand why this is happening."

She places a paw on my forearm. "You are not crazy, Kyra. Your memories should have returned already to you, but it seems they will take time."

"Memories of what?"

"Your past life," she explains as if it's such a simple matter. "In the Otherworld—Lunaria."

"But, I—"

"Please," she begs as she stands and gestures to the door. "Take me back to the café. Together we will speak with Cael. He holds the key to all of this."

I shake my head. "I don't understand. What does he have to do with all of this?"

"Trust me." She places a paw on my knee. "Soon, you will know everything."

Still not sure if I'm crazy or dreaming, I figure I may as well go along with this. But as we walk to the café, I'm not sure why I'm listening to a talking cat. Maybe I'm in shock. Or maybe I've really lost it. Claire is always pressuring me to get out more, to make friends, and even find someone. Instead, I preferred to keep to myself, spend every day in a café, typing away so I can get all the stories in my head out into the world.

My mind keeps circling back to all my stress about this current book. Yes, that has to be it. I'm simply stressed and this is my overactive imagination bubbling over and making me see and hear things. That's got to be it. I hope.

As soon as I enter the café, Cael's eyes meet mine from behind the counter. It's early, so I'm the first customer here. I don't see Aris, but I hear sounds coming from the back and assume he must be in the kitchen, preparing the pastries for the early morning rush.

"Hey, Kyra!" Cael greets me with a handsome smile. "You're here early."

I give him a nervous grin in return. "Yeah, there's uh…" I'm about to tell him there's something I want to talk to him about, but I lose my nerve. Instead, I move to the counter, meaning to place an order, but his warm teal eyes distract me.

A slow grin curves his mouth. "You want me to surprise you again?"

My cheeks heat under his intense gaze. "Yeah," I reply a bit breathlessly, then clear my throat as I come back to myself. "That would be great."

His gaze drops to Astra, her head and front two paws sticking out of my bag. "I see you brought your new companion today."

I glance down at her, astonished when the corners of her mouth quirk up in a smile, and she greets him.

"Hi, Cael."

My jaw drops.

"Hi, back. Would you like a bowl of milk?" he asks as if it's perfectly normal that a cat would be talking to him.

I lift my gaze to his and find him staring at me with a knowing look. My eyes roll up into the back of my head, and I fall away into darkness.

CHAPTER 6

KYRA

My mind slowly comes back to awareness as the smell of bacon fills the air. A sizzling sound tells me it's cooking on a stove somewhere. My eyes snap open to an unfamiliar room. Covered by a thick green fluffy comforter, I'm surrounded by a masculine scent, a cross somewhere between fresh rain and forest. Oddly appealing, I breathe it in deep.

I realize it's coming from the bedding. I dart a quick glance around the room. The walls are a pale, calming green, with several paintings of nature scenes. I'm in a four-poster bed with intricate carvings of vines and flowers etched into the rich, red colored wood.

Panic fills me. Where am I?

I lift the comforter and breathe a deep sigh of relief when I find I'm still completely clothed—a good sign. I hope it means I didn't do anything crazy like sleep with a stranger. I drop my head onto the pillow, struggling to remember how I got here. What the hell is going on?

"Are you all right?" Astra stares down at me, along with a fluffy white fox.

I blink and shoot up in the bed, grabbing Astra in my arms and holding her tight to my chest.

"Get back!" I yell at the strange white fox.

Its blue eyes stare at me with an almost puzzled look.

"It's all right, Astra," I tell her. "I won't let him eat you."

The fox purses his lips, appearing offended by my statement. "Why would I eat a cat when I'm about to have bacon?" He rolls his eyes, then turns, jumps off the bed, and saunters into the hallway as he glances over his shoulder. "Really, you humans are so strange."

I blink several times as I stare in shock at the far wall. Astra wriggles out of my grasp and places a paw on my hand, drawing my attention back to her.

"I know you think this is all some kind of dream, Kyra, and I'm sorry you're being introduced to all of this so… quickly."

I swallow nervously, then swing my legs over the bed.

"Where are we?" I ask, figuring if I'm still dreaming, I might as well ask questions so I can figure out how to wake up that much sooner. "Please tell me I didn't do anything embarrassing."

"We're at Cael's apartment," she replies. "He brought you here after you passed out at the café."

"All right." I drop my head into my hands and run my fingers roughly through my hair. "I remember going to the café, and…" I level an accusing glare at Astra. "You started talking to Cael, and I passed out."

Astra shrugs. "What was I supposed to do? Be rude and not say anything to him?"

Speechless, I stare at her in astonishment a moment before I stand. Moving quietly, I make my way down the hallway. Soft jazz, mellow and discordant notes, drift through the room.

I walk into the living area. It's finely furnished with a long L-shaped sofa, thick, plush green cushions, and a piano that sits in one corner of the room. It's connected to the kitchen, separated only by a long black granite counter. Cael's back is to me, his sleeves rolled up his forearms, as he stands before the stove, cooking bacon in a pan over the heat.

The white fox sits on the counter beside him. As if sensing my presence, it turns, and its bright blue eyes meet mine, then it leans toward Cael and whispers in his ear.

Cael spins to face me, greeting me with a wide smile.

"You're awake! Thank goodness."

"Um… what am I doing here?" I ask the most obvious question.

"I brought you here after you fainted in the café. Aris would have come too, but it was right before the morning rush, and he knows the ins and outs of the café much better than I do and—"

I lift my hand in a bid to allow me to speak. "What I mean is… why did you bring me here?"

He gives me a concerned look. Moving the pan off the burner, he walks over to me, and his teal eyes meet mine intently.

"I promise you I would never do anything to harm you in any way. I just wanted to take care of you, make sure you were all right." He gestures to Astra, then back to the fox. "When I first met my familiar, it was a shock for me, too. Aris as well," he adds. "So, I thought it would be good to bring you here to meet Lynx." He gestures again to the fox. "I'll do my best to answer any questions I can. I was hoping you might have some answers for me as well."

"Me?" I ask incredulously. "What kind of answers?"

His brow furrows softly. "When you found Astra, is that the first time anything… magical has ever happened to you?"

"Magical?" I blink several times as I process his words. "Yes. I don't recall having encountered any magic before…" I gesture to Astra.

"Okay." He smiles. "How about a cup of coffee, and we'll talk about all this?"

"I…" I open my mouth to protest, then decide to just go with it. If I'm going to go crazy, I might as well go all in. "That would be great."

He nods and moves back to the kitchen. I notice he has a machine similar to the espresso maker they use at the café. The delicious, rich smell of coffee fills the air as he prepares our drinks. When he comes back to the living room, he hands me a steaming mug.

"Careful," he warns. "It's hot."

I make sure to grab the handle to keep from burning my hand. I lift it to my nose and inhale deeply, drawing in the smell of cinnamon, chocolate, and caramel.

He smiles. "It's similar to what I gave you yesterday."

I take a small sip, releasing a low throaty hum as the warm liquid rolls across my tongue in a decadent burst of intense flavor.

He arches a brow. "What do you think?"

"It's wonderful. Thank you."

He leans toward me a bit, and my breath hitches. For a moment, I think he is going to kiss me. Instead, his eyes flick to my mouth before locking with mine.

"You're surprisingly calm about all of this."

I sit back in the chair and take another sip of my drink as I shrug. "It's just a dream, right? So I might as well just go with it."

He frowns. "Is that what you think this is?"

My brow furrows. "It's… not?"

"It's real, Kyra." He gestures to Lynx and Astra. "They're real too."

I take another sip of my coffee, allowing his words to sink in.

Astra jumps up on the chair beside me and places her paw on my hand. "I'm sorry this is all so shocking for you, Kyra."

Lynx dips his chin in a subtle nod. "I am as well." He looks to Cael. "I am glad you have finally found each other."

Cael narrows his eyes at Lynx. "What do you mean? What have you been holding back from me?"

The fox purses his lips. "What I have withheld from you has been for your own good. There are things you must discover on your own."

"Like what?" I ask, desperate to make sense of all this.

Astra steps forward. "You," she says, looking at me, "were a queen thousands of years ago in the Otherworld, and you," she adds, looking at Cael, "were her guard."

Even as she says it, I remember what happened when Cael's fingers brushed against mine in the café yesterday. A flood of images moved through me—specifically, the ones of the man holding me as I die in my nightmare. I reached for his face, telling him he was not to blame for my death, but there was something else this time. Something more… intimate. My heart ached, not because I was dying, but because my death meant I would leave him, which was the last thing I wanted to do. But why did I feel that way?

Instead of asking that, I choose a safer question. Besides, I don't want to bring up the images I saw or the feelings attached to them until I understand a bit more about what we're dealing with.

"What is the Otherworld?"

Lynx turns to me. "It is called Lunaria. A world parallel to this one but different in that it is controlled by magic."

"So, what does that have to do with us?"

Lynx gives me a solemn look. "All of the recent earthquakes lately… they are happening because the God of Destruction has escaped his prison and is looking for revenge. He wants to bring devastation and ruin to this world and to Lunaria."

"What?" I stare at him in disbelief. "Assuming this is all somehow real… what does that have to do with me?" I glance at Cael. "With us?"

"I was getting there," Lynx sighs heavily. "Now if you will kindly allow me to explain."

"I'm listening."

He continues. "Thousands of cycles ago, you were both Guardians of the God of Creation. It was your job to protect the five gemstones that controlled the elements. You used them to maintain the balance between this world and Lunaria."

"But there are only four elements," Cael interjects.

Lynx shakes his head. "There are five. Fire, Spirit, Earth, Water, and Wind. And if the God of Destruction gets ahold of them before we do, he will bring devastation and ruin to both worlds. It will be unlike anything ever seen before."

"Lunaria and Earth are linked together by a magical bond that was forged thousands of years ago," Astra explains. "Long ago, the first Queen of Lunaria opened a portal to Earth. She created a treaty between the two worlds by marrying Earth's King."

I give her a puzzled look. "When did Earth have a King that ruled the entire world?"

"Long before your written history," Lynx interjects.

Cael leans forward. "So what does this have to do with us?"

He looks to Cael. "You were a guard in your past life. A knight sent from Earth, in a gesture of friendship and peace, to help guard the future queen of Lunaria." Lynx shifts his gaze to me. "That was who you were, in your past life, Kyra."

Astra steps forward. "You were Guardians of the God of Creation. You maintained the balance between Destruction and Creation by wielding the power of the elemental gemstones. And now you have both been reborn in this world. Now that you have been reunited, you must return to the Otherworld—Lunaria—and retrieve the missing gems."

"Why are they missing? What happened?" I ask.

Astra shakes her head. "I do not know. I only know you are meant to find them and restore the Balance once more between our two worlds. Once you find the gemstones, you will control their power. Only then, can you force the God of Destruction back into his prison. But you must find the gems before his Guardians do first."

"Why are you only telling me all this now?" Cael stares accusingly at Lynx.

Lynx gives him a regretful look. "I would have told you sooner if I could, Cael. But I had to wait until you found her." He gestures to me. "She is the only one who can wield the power of the gemstones. And it is your duty to help her find them and protect them. You will need them for the war that is to come."

Frustration burns through me. I feel like I have more questions now than answers and I hate being kept in the dark. "What war? You're not making sense. I feel like you're just giving up pieces of the story but not the entire picture. Why is that?"

A sly smirk crests Lynx's lips. "You are just as you were before, my queen. Ever perceptive and always impatient."

"Stop answering my questions with riddles," I snap. I stand from my seat and begin pacing. "I feel like I'm going crazy. There are talking animals." I gesture to Lynx and

Astrid. "And I'm in some guy's apartment who I barely know and—"

Cael stands and rests his hands on my shoulders, meeting my gaze evenly.

"Hey, it's all right. I know it's a lot. I've been there. When I first met Lynx, I thought I was going crazy, too. And when Aris met his familiar, he thought—"

"Aris went through this, too?"

He smiles and nods. "That's kind of how we became friends. All this weird stuff happened to us, then these animals showed up, and…"

I narrow my eyes. "Did you know?"

"Know what?"

"When you rescued Astra," I tell him. "Did you know then?"

He shakes his head. "It wasn't until I touched you, I…" He stops and looks down at his hands. "I don't understand why, but when I touched you yesterday, it brought back images of my dreams and a recurring nightmare."

I inhale sharply as I meet his eyes evenly. "Does a woman die in your dreams?"

"You have the same nightmare," he says, his voice barely a whisper as he stares at the floor with a faraway look. "The same one that Aris and I have." He turns to Lynx. "What are you not telling us?"

Lynx sighs as he darts a glance at Astra before turning back to us.

"We cannot explain why there are three of you who share this same dream, but we *do know* why you have it."

"Why is that?" I ask, desperate to understand.

"It is because—" He stops abruptly, and his head whips to the door, his expression turning to one of alarm. "They're coming!" He looks to Astra. "We have to send them! Now!"

Her eyes snap to us. "Follow me!"

"What—" Cael starts to ask, but she cuts him off.

"There isn't time! You have to trust us."

Astra runs down the hallway to the bedroom, and we follow after her.

"What's going on?" I ask, but she doesn't answer.

Instead, she stands in front of the full-length mirror and bows her head, closing her eyes as she begins speaking words in a language I don't understand, but that somehow sound familiar.

Our reflections begin to waver as a soft shimmering glow surrounds the frame. Our images ripple and distort and then fall away completely, revealing a forest. A deafening sound splits the air behind us.

"They've forced the door!" Lynx cries out. "Send them now! We'll follow when we can."

"Send us where?" Cael asks in alarm. "What are you—"

"There isn't time!" Astra says, motioning for us to move to the mirror. "Step through the portal. Go to the Otherworld. You must locate the gemstones. Go! We'll find you."

"But I—"

She looks to Cael. "If you don't go, she'll die in your arms again just like before."

His eyes dart to mine, full of alarm. He takes my hand and pulls me toward the mirror. I try to jerk away, but he steps through. My jaw drops and I only have a moment to scream before I'm pulled through the portal.

Everything goes dark. Time slows as we float, suspended in nothingness.

"Where are we?"

He opens his mouth to answer, but everything speeds back up, and we're falling. We tumble through a darkened void. A terrified scream escapes my throat, and Cael grabs my flailing arms. Pulling me to him, he wraps his arms tightly around me.

"I've got you, Kyra."

I blink, and we slam to the ground. Cael takes the full brunt of the impact as I land on top of him.

Slightly dazed, I lift my head and notice we're in a forest. It must be the same one we saw in the mirror. Tall trees tower overhead, their gray trunks twisting toward the sky as if competing for the light of the sun. They are heavily laden with thick, purple, heart-shaped leaves. Long trailing vines with glowing white flowers hang down from their branches like living curtains, swaying gently in the breeze.

The ground is soft as I roll off Cael and onto the ground beside him.

He groans. "Are you all right?"

I wince inwardly. "Thanks to you. I'm sorry I fell on you."

"Better me than you." He gives me a lopsided grin. "According to Lynx and Astra, *I'm* only a guard, but *you're* the queen."

A small laugh escapes me, but my expression quickly sobers as I sit up. "Where do you think we are?"

Cael sits up beside me, his eyes scanning the thick woods that surround us. "I don't know. Astra was talking about the Otherworld—Lunaria. Maybe that's where she sent us."

He slowly stands and then reaches a hand down to pull me up. The moment my palm touches his, a flash of memory flits through my mind of us kissing in a forest just like this one.

He lays down beside me in a thick blanket of grass. I smile as he reaches across to brush a stray lock of hair back from my face, staring at me with a look of intense love and devotion. "You are mine, Alora," he whispers.

The vision fades and Cael's eyes meet mine, widening slightly.

"Did you see something just now when we touched?" I ask a bit hesitantly.

He nods and something unspoken passes between us as we stare at each other intently. If all this is true, and part of me is still doubting… believing somehow I'll wake up in my bed. I think Cael was more than just my guard.

Astra's last words replay in my mind: *If you don't go, she'll die in your arms again just like before.*

Cael is the man in my dreams who holds me as I lie dying. As he looks to me, everything about him feels so familiar. A deep ache settles in my chest and it's the same feeling I have in the dream as he stares down at me. I'm not sad or scared for myself. My heart always breaks for *him*—the man who holds me.

I open my mouth to speak but a strange animal noise startles us both. Whatever it is, it does not sound familiar at all.

Cael turns his gaze to the forest. "We're definitely not in Seattle."

A small huff of air escapes my lips as I stare up at the trees again with their long, trailing vines with softly glowing white flowers. "Definitely not Seattle."

I sigh heavily as my mind struggles to process what just happened. It's dark, and everything is new and unfamiliar. I'm not sure how safe it would be to go stumbling through the woods in the darkness, searching for civilization or shelter. I turn to Cael.

"I think we should just stay here for the night. In the morning, we can search for… something."

He nods. "I agree."

CHAPTER 7

KYRA

We're surrounded on all sides by a dense forest. With rich green and purple leaves and vibrant flowering plants with blooms that glow in the dark, I would think all of this is lovely if I wasn't so scared.

The night sky is clear above us and full of stars. I study them, hoping to spot a familiar constellation. But the ones I memorized as a child are not here. So wherever this is… it's far from home.

Cael guides me behind a row of thick and towering bushes, shielding us from any unwanted eyes. It's not much of a hiding spot, but it's better than nothing. At least we're in the shadows instead of in the light provided by the glowing flowers that hang down from the many trees.

A cool breeze blows through the forest, and I shiver slightly. Cael wraps his arm around me and tugs me into his side.

"Thanks," I whisper as I nestle against the solid warmth of his body. I lift my gaze to the sky again, surprised that I can see so many stars. In the city, it's almost impossible to see anything beyond the harsh glow of the streetlights and buildings. But here, there are so many stars, and they are so bright, it's incredible.

My mom always used to tell us that we should look for the good in every situation. So, despite my fear, that's exactly what I'm doing. I'm trying to appreciate the beauty and wonder of this strange world, attempting to ground myself in this moment.

I may be afraid, but I have to push down my anxiety and focus. Panic will not do either of us any good here. In the morning, we can figure out where we are and come up with some sort of plan.

Astra said she and Lynx would follow us here. So, we'll have to trust that they will. But until then, we need to keep our heads.

We lie back on the soft blanket of grass. The ground is a bit spongy beneath us, so it's not entirely uncomfortable. Despite being in a strange new world, I'm not as worried as I probably should be. I glance at Cael. Maybe it's because I'm not alone. Besides, there's something about him that makes me trust him. I don't know what it is beyond intuition. I've always been one to trust my instincts, and right now, they're telling me Cael is a good guy.

I turn to face him.

He gives me a faint smile. "Are you warm enough?"

It's hard to answer without my teeth chattering. "Not really."

"I'm cold too." He spreads his arms wide in invitation, and then gives me a teasing grin. "I promise I won't bite."

I move into the circle of his arms. He pulls me close to his chest. He's so warm, it's like lying next to my own personal heater, and I love it. I draw in a deep breath as I nestle into him. His masculine scent surrounds me, and it feels so comforting.

I can hardly believe I'm doing this. I've never even slept next to a guy before. Not that I haven't had offers to sleep with someone… It's just I never found anyone I liked enough to get that close to.

"Is this all right?" he asks.

I love that he's worried about my comfort level. That's so considerate of him.

"Yes. You?"

He nods.

He shifts and turns toward me, wincing slightly in pain.

I stare at him in concern. "How badly are you hurt?"

"Not bad. I'm just a bit sore from the landing."

"Thank you for that. For holding me and making sure I was safe."

"Of course," he replies softly.

I rest my head on his shoulder.

"You said you've been with Lynx for the past few years and mentioned Aris had a…" I pause, searching for the right words before finally settling on, "familiar as well."

He chuckles. "You make it sound crazy."

"Well, isn't it? I mean, just a bit, right?"

He shrugs. "I guess. I've just lived with it for so long, it feels pretty normal at this point."

"So, what kind of animal does Aris have? Is it a fox as well?"

"No, he has a peacock."

A soft laugh escapes me. "A peacock?"

"Yeah." He chuckles. "I know it sounds pretty unimpressive compared to a fox, but they're a good match, I think."

Now that I think about it, he's right. Peacocks are beautiful with their dazzling feathered display—the models of the bird kingdom. Aris is very handsome, so it's only fitting that he'd be paired with a peacock.

"They have psychic abilities, he and that bird of his," Cael says, a bitter edge to his tone.

I prop myself up on one elbow and grin down at him. "That bothers you?"

"I definitely can't keep any secrets from him." He rolls his eyes in mock frustration. "It makes it really hard to surprise him on his birthday. All they have to do is touch someone, and they know pretty much everything about them."

"Wow. That has to be overwhelming."

"I think it is for him. I mean, he has to be so careful around people. The last thing he wants is to touch them and violate their privacy." He pauses. "That's how we met. We bumped into each other, I knocked him down, and he took my hand to help him up without thinking."

My eyes widen. "What happened?"

"He saw my nightmare, the one I've been having for the past several years. And that's how I found out that he has it too." He sighs heavily. "It's terrible; I hate it."

I shrug. "Try being the one who dreams she's the woman that is dying."

His eyes snap up to meet mine, his gaze full of concern as he reaches out to cup my cheek, gently brushing the soft pad of his thumb across my skin. "That must be so awful for you."

"It is." A slight shiver runs through me at the memory, and he hugs me even tighter.

"I'm sorry," he whispers into my hair. "If my part in it is bad, I can only imagine how terrible it must be for you to dream that you are her."

"But I *am* her," I counter. "At least, according to Astra and Lynx."

His brows knit together in contemplation. "And I'm him. Or… maybe I'm not." He shakes his head as if frustrated. "I don't know because Aris has the same dream. And we can't both be that same person."

"That doesn't make any sense," I say, more to myself than to him.

"Does any of this?" He gestures to the sky and the forest around us. "This is all so… much more than I thought it would be." He pauses. "For so long, I've searched for answers but have yet to find any. The only thing I've ever found before now is Aris and Lynx."

"You and Aris sound like you're really close."

"We're like brothers." He pauses. "And he understands me. Both of us grew up without our parents. They died when we were young. We know what it's like to be alone."

I open my mouth to speak, but he beats me to it.

"I'm not complaining. I mean, I know there are worse things in life, and at least I had a roof over my head, but I never really had the one thing I always wanted."

"And what was that?"

"A family." Staring at the sky, he releases a soft sigh. "So, now Aris is my family, and I'm his."

My heart clenches, and I hug him a bit tighter. "I'm sorry you had such a lonely life until…"

"You don't need to feel sorry for me." His lips quirk up at the edges in a ghost of a smile. "I'm fine, but *you* should probably get some sleep. Who knows what tomorrow will bring."

I realize he's changed the subject to avoid discussing something obviously painful, but I don't press any further. Instead, I agree and rest my head on his shoulder again.

"What about you? Are you going to sleep?"

He nods. "I'll stay awake for a bit just to make sure everything's okay."

"I could take the first watch." I offer, knowing that instead of sleeping, my mind is probably going to be replaying everything that happened today.

He shakes his head. "According to Lynx, I'm *your* guard, remember?" he says with a sly smirk. "So, I need to stay awake… guarding, don't you think?"

"Fine. I'll sleep while you guard me. By the way," I tease, "do you even know the first thing about guarding?"

He shrugs. "It can't be that hard."

"Oh, really?" I arch a brow at him. "What makes you so sure?"

He flexes his opposite arm, showing off a very impressive bicep as he gives me a teasing grin. "Who would dare try to mess with this?"

I laugh, and his expression falls.

He narrows his eyes, but I note the faint smile that tugs at his lips. "You know, you're not exactly building my confidence here when you laugh at me like that."

"Sorry." I chuckle. "You're right. Anyone would be intimidated by you." I lightly squeeze his bicep for mock emphasis, and I'm astonished by the thick, corded muscle beneath his shirt. He's right. People should be intimidated by him. He's really built, his entire body a solid wall of muscle. I should know—I'm snuggled up against it.

My thoughts turn to our familiars. "Do you think Lynx and Astra will find us?"

"I'm sure of it. Lynx is nothing if not persistent. He always manages to talk me into making him bacon with every meal."

I laugh as I think of the sassy fox. "You two are really close, aren't you?"

"Yeah." A wistful smile crests his lips. "He and I argue, but it's mostly playful banter. I mean, you met him. You saw how he is." He laughs, but his expression quickly sobers. "To be honest, I miss him. He's family to me. Just like Aris."

I take his hand in mine as we lie staring up at the night sky.

"I may not remember everything, but this," he looks to

me, gently squeezing my hand. "It feels familiar somehow, doesn't it?"

"It does," I agree.

What I don't tell him is that it bothers me. It's unsettling to have these emotions and not really understand where they come from. I know Astra and Lynx say they're from a past life, but they still feel like a dream instead of something I actually lived. I look to Cael. "How much do you remember about your past life?"

"Only bits and pieces. It's like a—" he stops, his brow furrowing deeply as if searching for the right words before finally saying, "a heavy fog is surrounding my memories. I know they're there, but I can't seem to access all of them."

I sigh. "I feel the same. I get these fleeting images and then… they're just gone and I can't get them back. I don't even really know where they came from. It all still feels like some sort of strange dream."

"Maybe we'll find the answers in this place," he offers.

"I hope so."

A thought occurs to me and I turn to face him. "When did you start having the nightmares?"

"A little over five years ago. You?"

"The same," I reply. "What about Aris?"

"His started then too." He frowns. "It's like some sort of clock, isn't it? Like each of us suddenly started getting these memories all around the same time. How strange," he murmurs, and I realize he's speaking more to himself than to me. "I wish Lynx and Astra were here to explain it all. All these years and I was finally getting some answers."

Deep down, I worry Lynx and Astra may have been hurt, but I don't let myself dwell on the possibility. I have to hold out hope that they'll find us. Because if they don't, I have no idea how we're going to find the gemstones we are supposed to be searching for, or how we're going to get home.

"You should rest while you can," Cael whispers. "I won't let anything happen to you."

Even as he speaks words of reassurance, I wonder at him making this promise; telling me that he'll protect me. But as I lie in his arms, I feel safe. He's right. This feels so familiar, being this close to him, wrapped up in his embrace. As if it's the most natural thing in the world, despite the fact that we only recently met.

With a heavy sigh of exhaustion, I close my eyes and force myself to push aside these thoughts. I'm not going to get any more answers tonight and I need to rest. "All right. I'll try. Goodnight, Cael."

"Goodnight, Kyra."

As I allow myself to drift away, I fall back into my nightmare.

A man takes my hands. "We have to go! Now!" he yells.

Terror fills me as he pulls me behind him. We race down a long hallway. An angry mob surrounds us on all sides, but he somehow manages to cut a path through them with his sword.

He glances over his shoulder at me and I cry out as a man sinks a blade deep into his side. "No!"

CHAPTER 8

CAEL

Still asleep, Kyra nestles even closer to me as if instinctively seeking warmth and comfort in my arms. Despite the darkness, the glowing flowers around us cast just enough light that I'm able to see her without difficulty. I reach out and lightly brush the hair back from her face as I study her features. Her long, silken blond hair is spread out beneath her like a beautiful halo. Long lashes are fanned over soft pink cheeks and her lips are partially open in a small *o*.

Fierce protectiveness fills me as I observe her. She is beautiful—her face angelic as she sleeps. Her small brow furrows softly and I wonder if she is dreaming.

An image from my nightmare flashes through my mind and I inhale sharply as I recognize the terrible dream.

A small whimper escapes her as a tear slips down her cheek. Gently, I touch her shoulder to wake her. "Kyra?"

Her eyes snap open. She draws in a shaking breath.

"Are you all right?"

She turns her gaze to me and then softly shakes her head. "You saw it too, didn't you?" she whispers.

I nod and then wrap my arms tighter around her, pulling her close. "It's all right. It was just a nightmare."

Blinking back her tears, her blue eyes meet mine evenly. "No, they're not. These aren't just dreams, Cael. They are memories. I saw you get hurt. You were trying to protect me. Someone stabbed you and I couldn't do anything but watch." With a slight clench of her jaw, she turns her gaze up to the sky. "I hate this. It was bad enough when I thought these dreams were just recurring nightmares. But now that I know they were real…"

"I know," I speak softly. "It's a lot to process."

She shakes her head. "It's not just that, Cael. I… I have these feelings and these emotions, and I don't know if they're mine or if they were hers."

"I feel the same way," I murmur. "I have this overwhelming need to protect you, and comfort you, and—" I stop just short of saying "love you," because I don't know how she'll react to that. "It's just… strange to have these memories that are mine and yet… they aren't. Not of this life, anyway."

She nods.

In truth, it doesn't matter to me if these emotions are mine or not. As soon as we arrived here, more of the memories of my past life started coming to me. It's as if a floodgate was opened in my mind the moment we came to this world.

I wrap an arm around Kyra and pull her close, not just because I want to comfort her but because deep in my soul I feel connected to her. I feel like she's mine. And I'm hers. I know Lynx and Astra said I was her guard, but as I gaze down at her, nestled against my side, I know now we were much more to each other than just queen and guard.

She was mine and I was hers. I know this, but I do not

think she has remembered it yet. And until she does, I'm reluctant to bring it up because in this life… we're basically still strangers to one another.

I've had five years with Aris and several with Lynx. All of this is not entirely new to me like it is to her. I remember how overwhelming it all was when I first discovered that Aris and I shared the same nightmare. Things became even more so when I found Lynx.

She lifts her gaze to me. "I think I'm going to try to get some sleep."

A cold wind whips through the forest and she shivers against me as I hold her close. "I'll stay awake for a while and keep watch."

She closes her eyes. "Thank you, Cael."

I wrap my arms tight around her. Kyra is completely new to all of this. Despite what we may have been to one another in our past life, what she needs is a friend right now. And I want nothing more than to be whatever she needs.

CHAPTER 9

CAEL

When we wake in the morning, Kyra is still wrapped up in my arms. Half-asleep, I gently nuzzle her hair, breathing deep of her delicate scent. I note a soft hint of jasmine in the long, silken strands.

One of the abilities I picked up when I first linked with my familiar was a heightened sense of hearing, sight, and smell. Whereas, Aris's touch telepathy grew stronger after he found Fin. I wonder what abilities Kyra may have picked up now that she has found Astra.

A sharp snap draws my attention and I immediately train my ears toward the forest. Closing my eyes I focus, listening intently. The soft crunch of leaves underfoot tells me that someone is trying very carefully to be quiet as they approach our location.

Cautiously, I lift my head and scan the area, but see nothing. Whoever it is, they are far enough away that my keen vision cannot see them. I'm not sure why there is someone in the woods here with us, or if they are even searching for us in particular. I only know that I'd rather not allow them to find us before we can determine if they're friend or foe.

I lean down and whisper softly in Kyra's ear. "Be as quiet as you can. Someone is coming."

Her eyes snap open, panic and fear visible in their blue depths.

"Do not worry. They are far enough away, they have not seen us. We still have time to hide."

She nods, and we sit up. Quietly, we move deeper into the woods. When I'm satisfied we're not only downwind from whoever is approaching but also hidden well enough that they cannot spot us, we stop and crouch low in the underbrush.

Kyra turns to me. "Shouldn't we keep going?" she whispers.

I scan the area and then shake my head. Behind us is a river. We may be able to cross it, but looks can be deceiving. I don't know how deep it is nor how well Kyra can swim. The current doesn't look very fast, but I don't want to chance it. No. Our best bet is to hide and hope that whoever this is, will keep moving.

"They have to be close," a man's voice calls out. "I can sense it. Can't you?"

"I can," another answers. "If they are not here, they at least passed through very recently."

I peer through the thick leaves, trying to get a visual on these men. Whoever they are, they are not here by accident. Their words suggest as much.

I frown when I notice three men, dressed in dark pants and tunics with leather boots. They carry bows and arrows, of all things. I stare at them in astonishment. They appear as if they've just stepped out of a fairy tale about Robin Hood.

Kyra takes my hand as her gaze remains locked on our

pursuers. I squeeze it gently in return as we wait silently to see what they will do.

Whatever happens, I will protect her. I must. I turn to face her and whisper in a voice so low I'm sure the men cannot hear me. "If they find us, run to the river. Follow it downstream as fast as you can."

Her small brow furrows softly. "What about you?"

"I will find you."

She opens her mouth to argue, but I place a finger to her lips to silence her. I don't want to risk any further exchange and take a chance that the others may hear us.

I turn my gaze back to the men.

One of them studies the ground where we'd been lying only a moment ago. He kneels down next to the crushed grass. "They were here." He lifts his head, sweeping his gaze out over the forest as if searching for us. "We must find them... before the dark mages do."

Another one steps forward. "The High Mage said they'd be nearby. You know she's never wrong. So, that means they must still be close."

"Yes," another adds. "We must keep searching. If the dark mages find them, they will kill her guard and take the queen for themselves."

The queen. My heart stops as I think about what little Lynx and Astra told us of our former lives. If there was any doubt that these men were searching for us, it has now been completely erased. These men are speaking of myself and Kyra. They have to be.

As if sensing my thoughts, Kyra looks at me, indecision easily read in her expression.

"I don't know if I trust them," she whispers in a voice so low I almost miss it.

"I agree," I reply, equally as quiet. "Let's go."

She nods. Still holding her hand, I quietly lead her farther into the woods. Neither of us speaks as we make our way through the forest. Perhaps these men are good and actually mean us no harm, but I cannot risk it. Not until we know more about this world and why we are being hunted.

No. For now, I believe it will be safer for us to just stick together and find our own way. Hopefully, Lynx and Astra will come for us soon. I clench my jaw in frustration—that sneaky fox. All these years we've been together, he didn't say anything until last night. He spoke in riddles and half-truths. I could sense it. But why? Why would he not have told me about all of this sooner? And why not tell me the whole truth at the time? Why only give me bits and pieces of information?

I do not know. I only know when I see him again, he's going to have a lot to explain, and he'll be lucky if he ever sees another strip of bacon for the rest of his furry little life.

CHAPTER 10

KYRA

As soon as I think we're far enough away that it's safe to talk, I whisper to Cael. "Do you think they're following us?"

He stops and I go still as well. Cocking his head to one side, his brow furrows deeply as if listening intently for any sounds from the forest. After a moment, he shakes his head. "No. I no longer hear them behind us."

I blink up at him. "You're sure? How do you know?"

He nods. "When I first found Lynx, I somehow took on some of his... abilities."

"What do you mean?"

He shrugs. "I gained his super hearing and acute sense of sight and smell."

"Anything else?" I ask, as I scan him from head to toe, half expecting to see a furry tail or maybe even some fox ears peeking out from his head.

He laughs. "Not that I know of... yet." He scans me in

return. "What about you? Do you feel like you… gained anything after meeting Astra?"

I frown. "I don't feel any different. Did it happen right away for you with Lynx?"

"No."

I softly bite my lower lip as I consider what kinds of abilities I could gain from a cat. To be honest, it has me a bit worried. Well, that and everything else I suppose. I'm still trying to wrap my mind around all this past life stuff, and now we're being chased by strangers as well.

Drawing in a deep and steeling breath, I turn back to Cael. "Let's work on finding civilization—a town or a city. Maybe we can find somewhere safe to stay while we wait for Lynx and Astra to find us."

He nods, but I note that his attention is only half on me as his eyes continually scan the forest around us as if searching for any sign of danger. I don't complain though. With his foxlike gained abilities, he'll be able to alert us early of anyone coming our way. Hopefully that can help us avoid any unwanted company.

Cael suggests following the river and I agree. If this place is anything like where we came from, cities and towns seem to spring up near places with water.

Sure enough, it doesn't take long to find a city. Several buildings made of white and gray colored stone with dark gray slate tiled roofs line either side of the river. Several bridges span across the water. This place looks like something straight out of a medieval fantasy.

A castle sits in the center, on a hill, making it stand out in sharp contrast to the structures that surround it. With high walls and guards posted along the four watch towers, it's a rather impressive sight to behold.

As we draw closer, I note all the streets and walkways made of neatly kept cobblestone that wind throughout the city. I'm surprised by how much it looks like some sort of medieval town straight out of a fairytale book.

Cael and I stay just at the edge of it all, remaining in the shadows beneath the thick canopy of trees as we observe. Several people dressed in simple dresses or tunics and pants gather in what looks like a marketplace, checking out the various shops and stands with vendors touting their food and wares. I note some of the people appear to be a bit more finely dressed in elegant gowns and clothing, indicating they are probably among the wealthy citizens of this place.

The smell of meat, spice, and something sweet I cannot quite place permeates the air, and my stomach begins growling. How long has it been since I've had anything to eat?

As hungry as I am however, there's no way we can just stroll into a place like this and not stand out. The way we're dressed, it's obvious we're not from around here. With those men trailing us, the last thing we need is to draw attention to ourselves.

As if reading my thoughts, Cael looks to me. "We need to find some new clothes, so we can blend in."

I scan the crowd. "How are we supposed to do that?" I reach into the pockets of my pants and come out empty. "I don't have any money, and even if I did, it's probably not any good here."

"We'll figure something out," he replies as he scans the area.

Across the way, near the edge of the city, lies a small house. It sits behind one of the larger buildings. Made of white and gray stone, I notice the roof is thatched instead of slate tiles. There are a few spots that appear to have been damaged from one too many storms, so I imagine these residents probably do not have very much money.

The garden behind the house is neatly kept and full of

flowering plants and what look like vegetables, but I cannot be sure since there is no equivalent for them back on Earth.

A line of clothes hangs out to dry and I note that there are at least two pairs of pants and tunics in the bunch. When Cael turns to me, I know exactly what's going on behind those mischievous teal eyes. The same thought crossed my mind for all of a second before I decided it's too risky.

"No," I tell him. "We can't steal anything."

He arches a brow. "Normally, I would agree, but right now, we don't have a choice. Even if we were to try to barter these," he says, gesturing to our clothing, "we would still be noticed, which is the last thing we want. We need to blend in, Kyra."

I sigh heavily. He's right. "I just... I hate the idea of stealing."

He places his hands on my shoulders and meets my eyes evenly.

"I don't like it either." He gives me a faint smile. "If it makes you feel any better, I'll do it. You wait here."

"What if you get caught?"

His gaze sweeps to the house once more. "Then, be my lookout. Give me a signal. Some kind of bird call or something if you notice anyone coming. All right?"

"Bird call?" I give him an incredulous look.

"You know... like: Caw-caw." He chuckles. "Or... something like that.

Amusement dances behind his eyes as I purse my lips. "Are you serious?"

He laughs softly. "Think of something else then... like a meow or—"

"I get it," I roll my eyes in mock frustration. "Just be careful, okay?"

"My familiar is a fox and I inherited some of his abilities."

He winks. "In my past life I was your guard. And foxes are sly. With those two powers combined, I think I'll be just fine."

I can't tell if he's actually this cocky or if he's feigning confidence for my sake. Either way, I'm still worried. I take his hand in mine and meet his gaze evenly. "All right, Mr. Sly Fox. Just be careful okay?"

He grins and then gives me a mock bow. "Of course, my queen."

I roll my eyes again, trying but failing to suppress a grin at his teasing.

He smiles in return, but his expression quickly sobers. "No matter what happens, I want you to stay hidden, all right? Promise me."

"Then promise you won't get caught," I counter.

"I won't." Despite his statement, I can see the worry behind his eyes. He's trying to be brave for me. "Any chance your guard could get a good luck kiss from his queen to send him on his way?" He teases.

I playfully slap at his arm as I shake my head. "Just be careful."

He nods and then turns his attention back toward his goal. With a quick glance to make sure no one is watching, he steps out from the forest and cautiously makes his way to the house.

Cael approaches the low garden wall, braces one hand on the stone, and then jumps over into the yard.

I hold my breath as he moves along the wall behind a row of bushes, trying to be as inconspicuous as possible. When he reaches the clothesline, he's about to remove the first tunic from the line when an old woman comes out the backdoor.

My heart stops, then begins hammering because I realize he hasn't noticed her since she hasn't turned the corner toward him yet. I gasp as she starts in his direction.

"Caw! Caw! Caw!" I cry out, sounding like anything but an actual bird.

Cael whips his head toward me as I gesture animatedly toward the woman. He rushes back to the line of bushes and ducks behind them, barely missing the woman as she turns the corner of the house and makes her way to the clothesline.

His teal eyes meet mine full of worry, but we both remain silent and still.

The old woman stops. Her gaze darts toward the bushes as she places her hands on her hips. "You can come out," she says. "I've been waiting for you, you know."

My mouth drifts open, and so does Cael's.

"I know you're there, Cael," she says. "And I know Kyra is as well."

I inhale sharply.

"Oh." She smiles, looking directly toward my hiding spot. "There you are."

Still in shock, I step out of the woods.

Cael moves in front of me, placing himself directly between me and the old woman. "Run, Kyra! Go back to the forest! I'll find you."

Panic tightens my chest. I can't leave him. Even if it means we're both caught.

The old woman smiles as she looks to him. "You are just as I knew you'd be. Protective of your queen."

I blink at her in confusion. "What are you—"

"I know who you are." She meets my eyes evenly before darting a glance at Cael. "And I know who he is. I have been waiting for you both. Come." She turns back toward the house.

When we don't follow immediately, she looks over her shoulder. "Or you can stay out here if you're not worried about being caught by people who would mean you both harm."

Cael turns to me, and I give him a subtle nod.

He narrows his eyes at the old woman. "If you try to harm her, I'll end you."

I stare at him, astonished at his words and his threat.

She nods and then continues on toward the house. "I do not doubt that."

As soon as I reach him, he holds out his arm motioning for me to stay behind him. "I'll go first," he whispers. "You run at the first sign of trouble."

I agree even though I have no intention of leaving him behind. No matter what.

Together, we follow the old woman back to her home.

As soon as we step through the door, the smell of fresh bread baking in the oven fills my nostrils. The space is small but cozy. Dried herbs hang on a rack over the counter, and a wood-fired stove is burning nearby. The wooden floors, walls, and ceiling are faded with age, the floor creaking with every other step as she leads us to the living area and a small fireplace in the corner.

The fire crackles as she stokes the flame. She throws another log on the hearth, turning it into a roaring fire as she gestures for us to take a seat on the sofa directly across the small table from her.

Everything in here appears to be worn with age, yet neatly kept. The entire place immaculately clean and organized. The cushions are a faded green but they are soft. I hadn't realized how tired and aching my legs and feet were until we're seated. But then again, we have been walking for a good part of the day through the woods.

The old woman is about to sit down when she stops herself and gives us an apologetic look.

"Forgive me," she says. "I'm a terrible host. Are you hungry?"

My first inclination is to say yes, but this woman is a

stranger, and I'm still not entirely sure we should trust her. I look at Cael, and I can read the same hesitation in his expression.

"I mean you no harm," she murmurs. "I have been waiting for you both for such a long time." Her lavender eyes meet mine. "Your coming was foretold many years ago."

"I… don't understand. You knew we were coming?"

"How do you know our names?" Cael asks, his voice hard and wary.

She gives us a warm smile, the fine lines of her face creasing at the edges of her eyes and mouth. If she's a bad person, her looks are deceptive. Her friendly appearance and the way she speaks in such a soft, lilting voice makes me inclined to trust her.

"I am Mage Willow," she introduces herself. "You have had a long journey, and it has only begun. Please, allow me to feed and shelter you this evening. It would be my greatest honor."

CHAPTER 11

KYRA

She walks into the kitchen and removes the bread from the stove. The fresh scent fills the air even stronger now, and my stomach growls, betraying just how hungry I am.

A pot on top of the stove draws my attention, and I watch as she ladles out three bowls of some sort of stew. Whatever it is, it smells delicious. She moves back to the living area and hands me the first bowl. Cael wraps his hand around my forearm to stop me from taking it. The moment his skin touches mine, a strange warmth emanates from the contact, and myriad images float to the surface of my mind.

Cael is lying in a bed beside me, his gaze locked on mine. He leans in and presses a tender kiss to my mouth that I return with equal fervor. "I love you, Bryndon," I whisper softly.

I can almost taste him on my lips, and I gasp. Cael relinquishes his grip and blinks several times as if coming back to himself. When his eyes meet mine, the image flashes again in my mind, and my mouth drifts open slightly.

77

"I—I don't understand."

The old woman chuckles. "The memories are beginning to return, it seems."

Our heads whip toward her.

"This is good. It will make what I have to tell you much easier."

A soft knock at the door draws our attention.

"Come in!" she calls out.

Cael jumps up and places himself between me and the door as if to shield me from a would-be attacker.

A woman enters, and her jaw drops when she looks at Cael and me. Her lavender eyes and long pale hair are a match for the old woman. I wonder if she is her daughter or some kind of close relation. As if in answer to my question, the old woman moves toward her and embraces her warmly.

Cael eyes them both warily.

"This is my daughter, Talina." She smiles at us, then arches a brow at her child. "He is just as I suspected he would be. As protective of his queen as the ancient stories told."

"Stop speaking in riddles, old woman," Cael grinds out. "Who are you? And how do you know us?"

"As I said. I am a mage." She places a hand on her chest. "So is my daughter. Your coming has been foretold for many years." A warm smile lights her face as she bows before us. "I am honored it was me you came to first. Now, please." She looks at Cael. "Know I would never harm you. I swear it to the God of Creation."

I place a hand on Cael's shoulder, forcing his attention back to me.

"Cael, I think we should listen to her."

"It could be dangerous," he counters. "We cannot risk—"

"We don't know where we are or why we're here." I meet his gaze evenly. "We might get some answers here, Cael. That's what we need, isn't it?"

With a slight clench of his jaw, he nods.

"Good." Talina smiles, having overheard us. "I'll make some tea."

Willow hands us each a bowl of soup. I'm so hungry, I eagerly eat mine, but I notice Cael hesitates. In fact, he waits so long, I'm already done with mine before he even takes his first spoonful.

Willow nods at him. "I respect you are cautious in regard to your queen. I do not think you will make the same mistake in this life."

"Mistake?" he asks.

She leans forward. "You have only recently come to this world, yes?"

"We… arrived here yesterday."

"And the world from which you have come does not possess any magic?"

"No," I reply.

Talina makes a soft tsking noise in the back of her throat, and then waves a hand in our direction. The bowls lift from our hands and move back to the kitchen, setting down on the counter near the sink. Her lips twist up in a sly smirk at our gaping stares.

"I've always wondered how the other side manages without the little things like this, which make life so much easier," she says. "I don't know what I'd do without my magic."

Cael and I remain silent, both of us in shock.

He leans forward. "Tell us everything you know."

CHAPTER 12

CAEL

Willow waves her hand, and a book flies from the shelf behind us. It is large and leather-bound, reminding me of an ancient tome. It alights on the table between us, and she carefully opens the worn and yellowing pages. At first, the symbols inside are completely foreign, but after a moment of staring at them, they realign into English, and I realize I can read them without difficulty. I blink several times as I stare down at the writings.

"How is that possible?"

I look at Kyra, her expression of wonder mirroring my own.

"You are the queen," Willow says to Kyra, "and you,"—she looks to me—"are her guard. So, of course, the light magic of this world will do everything it can to aid you in your quest to save it."

I grit my teeth. She is still speaking in riddles. I hate not knowing what's going on. I don't know if she is intentionally being cryptic, or if she is worried about telling us too much all at once.

After all, didn't Lynx and Astra do the same to us before we came here? I curl my hands into fists at my side at the memory. How long did that sly fox live with me, and all the while, he was keeping secrets? I'm tired of being kept in the dark.

"Tell us what you know," I demand. "Now."

Willow leans forward and looks to Kyra.

"In your past life, thousands of years ago, you were the Great Queen Alora—Ruler of both Earth and Lunaria. You were a Guardian of the God of Creation, just as all of your ancestors—the Great Queens—before you. You were tasked with keeping the dark mages and the Guardians of Destruction from destroying our two worlds. You fought those would have gladly seen our civilizations fall into chaos and ruin."

She turns to me. "And you were the queen's guard and protector. You were a knight from Earth—the most renowned and feared of any before you. You were sent here by the king of that world in a gesture of peace and friendship. You became a Guardian of Creation as well."

Kyra sits forward. "I've heard this place referred to as the 'Otherworld.' Why?"

"To those who live here, this is the world of Lunaria," Willow explains. "But to those who come from the place whence you came, it is known as the 'Otherworld.'"

"Why is that?"

"Because only those with magic can open a portal between the two worlds and pass freely from one to the other. As the queen reborn, I am not surprised you possess this ability."

Kyra and I exchange a knowing glance and remain silent, neither of us mentioning our familiars nor the fact that it was Astra who sent us here. After all, this woman may seem friendly, but it's best to remain cautious.

"What happened to her?" Kyra asks. "What happened to Queen Alora?"

Willow sits back in her chair and gives us a subtle nod before taking another small sip of her tea. "It seems your memories are far from returned. You speak of Alora as if you do not remember that you are her."

"I—" Kyra starts, but the old woman lifts her hand in a silent bid to be allowed to speak.

"Do not worry," she says. "The memories will come." She narrows her eyes as she looks to me. "It seems many of yours have returned to you, have they not?"

My mouth drifts open. How does she know? "How do you—"

She cuts me off. I look to the side and notice Kyra staring at me. Now she knows I've been keeping this from her. I lower my gaze, ashamed by the look of betrayal etched in her features. I'll have to speak with her when we're alone. I was only trying to give her time to adjust to all this. Now, I realize, from the look on her face that I should have just told her the truth.

The old woman is right. My memories are coming back. This world doesn't feel as foreign as it first did. If anything, it feels as if we've finally returned home.

Willow continues. "Like the ancient queens of old, Queen Alora was supposed to choose her harem—the men who would guard and protect her with their lives." Her gaze sweeps to me. "But she chose to only bond herself to one male. She was so in love with him, she refused all others who offered their hands. And that," she says sadly, "was her undoing."

I shake my head. "Why would she do that?"

Willow gives me a curious look. "You have experienced the nightmare of the queen's death, have you not?"

I blink several times, stunned that she knows this. "Yes."

"And yet, you do not remember the reason that the queen died?"

"Why would *I* remember?"

Her gaze hardens. "You were her guard. You were supposed to protect her." She studies me a moment. "How is it you do not have this memory?" Her gaze shifts to Kyra. "And you? Do you not remember what happened, either?"

Kyra frowns and shakes her head. "I have nightmares of dying, but they are like fragments of memory shrouded in fog. I cannot see more than that." She looks at me. "I only know when we touch, images flash through my mind. A man holds me in my dreams as I lay dying. And that man looks like Cael."

Willow frowns. "This is strange. You both are supposed to regain all your memories now that you are here."

"Perhaps it takes time, Mother," Talina offers.

"I still don't understand," Kyra says. "What does all this have to do with us now?"

Willow takes Kyra's hands. "I am forbidden from telling you everything. For there are things you must discover on your own. But I can tell you this: The balance of both worlds, this one and the one from which you have come, are linked. Destruction and Creation are two forces in complete opposition to one another. Thus, the gods have chosen their mages and their Guardians. The fact that the God of Creation made certain you were both reborn now means the God of Destruction is trying to rise to power once again."

"But you just said there had to be a balance," I interject.

"Yes, but the God of Destruction does not care to maintain it. He would destroy everything if he could. And you,"—

she points to me—"cannot allow that to happen. Protect the queen, and you save both worlds."

"What are you talking about?" Kyra asks. "This is crazy."

Willow tips up her chin and draws in a deep breath. "The world from which you come… have there been any destructive cycles?"

"Destructive cycles?" I ask, trying to understand what she's talking about. "What do you mean?"

She clenches her jaw. "Any disruption in the balance of nature. Unusual tempests or terrible quakes in the earth?"

Dawned understanding fills me. "The earthquakes," I whisper.

Kyra's eyes snap to mine. "They've been worse lately and no one understands why," she adds.

Willow looks between us both. "The same thing is happening here. It is the God of Destruction. Someone has managed to free him from his prison. And now he means to tear both worlds apart."

I shake my head, still having trouble wrapping my mind around all of this. "But why? Why would he do this?"

She shrugs. "It is his nature. He is the God of Destruction. He would see both our worlds burned and destroyed simply because it pleases him to do such a thing."

"But why now?" I ask.

She shakes her head. "*That*, I do not know. Nobody does. The will of the Gods is their own. Who knows why they do the things they do."

Kyra scoffs. "Assuming all of this is true. If I'm this queen you're speaking of, how am I supposed to save both worlds?"

Willow narrows her eyes. "It seems you still have doubts." She reaches across the table and takes both our hands. "Allow me to put them to rest."

The old woman closes her eyes and bows her head. Kyra

and I exchange a glance a moment before everything goes dark.

Panicked, I blink several times as if that will somehow help me to see. Myriad images fill my mind and my jaw drops as I watch the world burn all around me. Chaos, destruction, ruin and death. Both this world and the one we have come from. All of it is burning.

Buildings collapse and entire cities are swallowed by the earth as fire rains down from above, laying waste to the last vestiges of civilization. I turn to my left to find Kyra standing beside me. Her eyes wide in shock, a tear slips down her cheek as we stare at the wasteland that used to be our native city of Seattle.

"What happened here?" she turns to Willow as she stands before us.

"This," the old woman gestures to the ruin all around us, "is what will happen if the God of Destruction disrupts the Balance of all things. This is the death he would bring to both of our worlds."

She releases our hands and I blink as the room comes back into focus. I lower my gaze to the floor, struggling to process all that I've seen. I close my eyes, trying to force the terrible images from my mind, but I cannot. Kyra's hand covers mine and she squeezes it gently, drawing my attention back to her.

She meets the old woman's gaze evenly. "How do we keep this from happening?"

"Of all the Great Queens who came before you, you are the most powerful. You have the ability to wield all five of the elements. The queens before you were only able to wield one or sometimes two. But all of that magic is difficult to contain and control. That is another reason why the queens had their harems."

Kyra shakes her head. "I don't understand."

Willow continues. "The queen's mates had powers of their own as well. Not nearly as strong as what she possessed. The magic of the elements is a difficult thing to control. If one is not careful, they can be consumed by the destructive power of fire, spirit, earth, water, or wind. The harems always consisted of five men. Each one able to conjure the magic of a different element and to help their queen to wield it as well."

The old woman studies Kyra a moment and then looks to me. "Each of you has power. I can sense it. But it is not yet at full strength. You must find the hidden gemstones, the ones that fit the crown and allow you to wield complete control of the elements."

"What crown?"

"The one you were buried with in your past life."

An image of Alora wearing a crown flits through my mind, along with the memory of her lying in state with it on. A terrible ache settles deep in my chest as I recall dropping to my knees before the queen I had failed and offering an ocean of tears to the altar of my pain and despair.

I meet her gaze evenly. "How do we find the crown? How do we find the gemstones?"

Willow's sharp eyes meet mine. "You remember it, don't you?"

"Yes, but the memory of where the crown lies..." I pause, bracing myself to speak as agonizing grief moves through me before I finally say, "buried, is gone."

Although I do not entirely remember why or how it happened, I somehow know that I am responsible for Alora's death. I failed her somehow, and I never forgave myself for it.

Kyra looks to me, but I avert my gaze, unable to stare at her through my deep shame and guilt.

Talina leans forward and places her hand over mine. Her lips do not move. My eyes go wide as I hear her voice in my mind. *"Do not despair. The God of Creation did not blame you for what happened to your queen. If he did, he would not have allowed you to have been reborn to protect her now."*

Quickly I retract my hand, staring at her in shock.

Willow looks to us. "I will give you a map to the crown. Once you find it, it will lead you to the gemstones."

Willow gestures to the shelf behind me, and a scroll floats up from the stack of books on one level. I watch in awe as it gently lands on the table on top of the ancient tome. She unrolls it to reveal an intricately drawn and detailed map. Just like the tome, the parchment is yellowed and worn with age. I'm almost afraid to touch it. It looks as if it will fall apart from even the slightest breeze. Just as before, with the book, the words on the map morph into something I can read, and I study it curiously.

"Where are we on here?"

She points to a spot on the lower-left corner of the map called Aerondale. "This is us," she says. "And here,"—she trails her finger lightly on the map up toward the center—"is Valyra, the capital city. This is where Queen Alora was entombed."

A deep ache settles in the center of my chest as I look to Valyra and the space where the queen is buried. I dart a glance at Kyra. The urge to pull her into my arms is maddening. But I force myself to remain still because I do not think she'd welcome my touch. I cannot allow myself to forget that whatever we were to each other in a past life, we are still relative strangers in this one now.

It's frustrating since I do not know how much of what I feel for her is a memory of that life versus what little I know of her in this one. I look at Willow and Talina. I have so many things I want to ask them, but I hesitate. I'm both fearful and anxious to know the answers to my questions.

Why do I dream of holding the queen while she is dying? And why does it still hurt so badly when I dream of it? Her death was my fault. It must have been. Why else would I feel such guilt and pain when I think on it? I want to understand how I failed her, so I do not repeat this mistake again in this life, but I do not want to ask in front of Kyra because I fear the answer to my questions will be something terrible.

As if sensing my dark thoughts, Willow's eyes dart briefly to mine before she turns her gaze back to the fire.

The sun dips low on the horizon as night begins to settle in. The air grows colder as the wind picks up outside the house. She looks to the window. "It's fortunate you found me when you did. A terrible tempest is brewing outside. I believe it is a sign that the God of Destruction senses your presence in this world, now that you have returned."

"Will he find us here?" I ask.

She shakes her head. "You are safe this night. I swear it."

I have no choice but to take her word as I stare out the window and notice the dark clouds gathering overhead. A rolling boom of thunder shakes the house as lightning streaks across the sky. Rain begins falling in thick, heavy sheets, battering against the thin panes of glass.

Willow adds more wood to the hearth, stoking the fire until it turns into a roaring flame to warm the house. When she is finished, she leads us to the only bedroom in the cottage.

"Here." She gestures to the small bed in the corner of the room. "You may sleep in my room tonight. There's extra clothing in the dresser for you both."

My brow furrows and a smile tips her lips as she looks to me. "I knew you two were coming. It has been foretold for some time. So I made certain I had clothes for a man on hand."

Kyra nervously bites her lower lip as her gaze sweeps from the bed back to me.

Sensing her discomfort, I move to reassure her. "I'll take the floor. You can have the bed."

"You don't have to do that. You can have the—"

"No," I smile. "I insist."

Willow arches a brow. "The tub is full of hot water if you'd like to use it." She gestures to a room divider across the way.

I walk around the flimsy partition and notice the large clawfoot tub full of water just behind it but no obvious plumbing.

"How did you get the hot water?"

"Magic has many uses." She winks and wiggles her fingers.

"Ah," I reply. Of course, it does in a place such as this. "You will have to teach me some of that."

She blinks up at me. "You already possess magic of your own. Do you not feel it?"

I frown and look at my hands. "To be honest, no, I do not."

"It will come to you with time," she replies sagely. "I am certain of it."

When she leaves the room, I realize she hasn't left us any towels.

"I'll be right back." I tell Kyra. "Just need to get us some towels."

"All right," she replies as she sits on the edge of the bed.

When I go back into the living area, Talina is sitting on the sofa.

"Where is your mother? I was going to see if she had any towels we might use."

Talina's eyes move to the door. "She's outside, making sure the protective wards are in place." My brow furrows in confusion, so she explains. "They are barrier spells to keep out any who would mean you harm."

"That sounds… handy. Do you think you could teach me some of those wards or spells?" I ask, hopeful.

She nods. "You've not had practice, so they will not be as strong as what my mother or I can conjure, but it should be enough to allow you to sleep soundly during your travels."

"Thank you," I tell her. "So, how do we begin?"

She stands and moves toward me. Her lavender eyes search mine a moment before she takes both my hands. A soft glow emanates from the connection as warmth seeps through my palms at her touch. She closes her eyes, concentrating, and my mouth drifts open as words form in my mind, strange and not in any tongue I've ever heard before. It is as if they are being etched directly into my consciousness. Although I've never spoken them before, I am now able to speak them aloud, the lilting words strange but almost musical on my tongue.

A flash of memory flits through my thoughts. It's my nightmare, but different. Instead of holding the queen as she dies, I'm kneeling before her body, laid out in state. The ache in my chest is unbearable, and a tear slips down my cheeks, unbidden.

"What is this?" My voice comes out as barely a whisper as I struggle to choke back a sob. "Why do I feel this way?"

Talina reaches up to gently cup my cheek. "You remember mourning your queen," she whispers. "You were devastated because you blamed yourself."

"Why?" I ask.

She shakes her head. "There are things you much discover for yourself, my Lord."

The image returns and a man walks up beside me. His entire body glowing so brightly, it is difficult to look upon him.

She inhales sharply and pulls away, her eyes wide as she stares up at me.

"The God of Creation granted your request."

I shake my head softly in confusion. "What request?"

"You asked him for a favor, and he granted it."

"What favor? What are you talking about?" I do not remember speaking to the man.

"The God of Creation told you that you would both be reborn. You feared she would come to the same end if you were the only one she accepted into her guard, so you asked him for four others. Four guards that she would not refuse." Her brow furrows softly as she looks to me. "He granted your request."

"Where are they and how do I find them?"

"*They* will find *you*," she replies. "They are drawn to her light, just as you were."

Instantly, my thoughts turn to Aris. He has a familiar—Fin—and he has the same dreams of the queen that I do.

"Can you tell me anything else about them?" I beg, hoping she can give us a lead.

She gives me a pitying look. "I'm sorry. That is all I sensed."

"It's all right. It's more than we knew before. Thank you."

She nods and then retrieves two towels from a linen closet in the hallway. "Here. You may use these."

I take them from her and turn back toward the bedroom, but her small hand on my forearm stops me abruptly. "There is something you must know."

"What is it?"

"The Queen is the key to saving both our worlds. Whatever happens, she must be protected. Do you understand?"

"I would give my life to keep her safe."

She gives me a pained look. "Your life is an easy thing to give. But your heart is another matter entirely."

"I will do whatever it takes," I vow. "No matter the cost to myself."

She meets my eyes evenly. "Remember this when the time comes."

I give her a wary look. "What are you not telling me?"

She releases her grip on my arm. "I cannot tell you the things which you must discover for yourself. I am only allowed to give you warning."

"Warning? About what?" Frustration burns through me. "I'm tired of half-truths and riddles. Tell me what I need to know to protect her now. Please."

"It is not for me to tell. I vow that I do not withhold things from you without reason. It is part of the prophecy that you discover the answers for yourself."

Her lavender eyes stare up at me full of resolve, and it is easy to see she will not give me any more information.

After a moment, she dips her chin in a subtle bow and then turns back toward the living room.

When I return to the bedroom, I'm back to where I was before. With far more questions than answers.

Kyra is still sitting on the bed staring at the opposite wall with a faraway look on her face. I can only imagine how difficult this must be for her. She only just discovered Astra and now... all of this.

She lifts her gaze to me. "Why didn't you tell me that you were already regaining more of your memories?"

I clench my jaw as I sit down beside her. "The things I'm remembering..." I pause, uncertain how to continue. How do I tell her that I remember loving her? That I remember holding her in my arms? And that I know somehow I am responsible for her dying? "I was worried they might upset you."

She takes my hands, her blue eyes searching mine. "All we have here is each other. And yes, it's all a bit... overwhelming, but I'm not fragile, Cael, if that's what you think. I can handle things. I don't want any secrets between us, all right?"

I nod.

She gives me a faint smile. "How about we get cleaned up first and then we talk?"

I dread having to tell her about my memories, but I know that I must. She has asked that we not hold anything back from each other. "All right."

CHAPTER 13

CAEL

She moves behind the room divider, and I hear the soft rustle of her clothing as she undresses. She drapes it over the screen, and I swallow thickly. My every sense is completely attuned to her as I imagine her nude form behind the partition. A light rippling sound of water a moment later tells me she's in the tub.

"Cael?" she calls out. "Are you still there?"

"Yes." My voice is rough, even to my own ears. I clear my throat. "Do you need something?"

"No. I just… wanted to make sure you were still there."

"I am." I want to assure her that I will always be here. I pledged my life to her in the past and I will gladly do so again. But instead of saying this, I remain silent, uncertain if it is something she would wish to hear.

She bathes quickly and comes out wearing a long sleeping gown so threadbare, it hides almost nothing of her body. My gaze travels down her form, over the sensuous curve of her breasts and the gentle flare of her hips before I force myself to avert my eyes.

Before she has a chance to notice the obvious effect she is having upon me while she stands there in such little clothing, I move past her and quickly peel off my clothes and jump into the tub. Thankfully, the water is still warm.

I'm tempted to take my time, but I know she wishes to talk before we fall asleep. With a heavy sigh, I get out of the water and wrap a towel loosely around my hips. When I step around the partition, I cannot help but notice how Kyra's face flushes a charming shade of red as her gaze travels over my body.

As soon as she notices my eyes upon her, she looks away.

She hands me my clothes and I move back behind the partition. Quickly, I change into soft knit pants and a shirt almost as threadbare as Kyra's. When I come out from behind the screen, a smile tugs at my lips when I realize she's placed a pillow and blanket on the floor for me in a makeshift bed of sorts.

"Thank you," I tell her as I take my place on the floor.

She looks over the edge of the bed at me. "You're sure you don't want the bed?"

I grin. "What kind of gentleman would take the bed and make his companion sleep on the floor?"

She laughs. "You have a point." Her expression sobers. "Have you remembered anything else?"

"I spoke with Talina. She said we are supposed to find four other guards to help protect you."

"How do we locate them?"

"I do not know."

She gives me a hesitant look. "There's something I remembered… when we touched earlier."

"What was it?"

CHAPTER 14

KYRA

He stares up at me expectantly, waiting for me to answer, but I'm nervous about telling him. What I remembered felt so intimate. I must take too long to answer because he begins instead.

"We were very close in our other life. We knew each other before you became queen and before I became your guard."

I release the breath I hadn't realized I'd been holding, relieved he already knew what I was going to say.

"I remember that too," I whisper. What I do not tell him is that I believe we may have been lovers. I cannot be certain though because my memories are not whole. I only see bits and fragments of images and emotions, but there is no mistaking the pull I feel toward Cael.

It is not one to someone who is simply a friend. It feels like so much more. If he remembers this, he has said nothing… but, then again, neither have I.

He lifts his gaze to me, his eyes full of sadness. "I also

believe that my relationship with you had something to do with your death, but I do not understand what. I only know that I felt like I had failed you."

I still. "How do you know this?"

He places a hand to his chest. "I feel it here. And… Talina suggested as much when I talked to her."

"What did she say?" I ask, curious to understand.

Cael clenches his jaw as he looks down at the floor. "She spoke in riddles. Just like her mother and Lynx and Astra. She said there were things we needed to discover for ourselves."

"There has to be a good reason why Lynx never told you anything all these years." I pause and then lift my gaze to his. "When did you realize we had a connection?"

"To be completely honest with you, Kyra, when you first walked into the café the other day, I already recognized you somehow." He sighs. "I can't explain it. I just felt a… a pull to you. Then when we touched, images of my recurring dream flashed in my mind, and I… I knew it was you."

"I felt the same… I was drawn to you," I admit. "I mean, you look just like the man in my dream, but when we touched it was as if I knew for certain you were him. And I felt the connection then, but I… did not completely understand it." I pause, trying to think of the best way to explain, finally settling on, "Like a familiarity, a trust I shouldn't have so quickly with someone I just met. But… with you, I already do."

"I feel the same way." He gently tucks a stray tendril of hair behind my ear as his teal eyes stare deep into mine. "Whatever happens, I promise you… we'll figure this out together, Kyra."

"Do you think Astra and Lynx are all right?" The question has weighed heavily on my mind since we got here. They sent us through the mirror to save us, and I hope and pray they're all right. "I thought they would have found us by now if they were."

Cael grins. "If anyone knows how to take care of himself, it's Lynx. He's a sly one, that fox. I'm sure he and Astra are okay."

"How did you two meet?"

Cael lies on his back and places his hands behind his head as a smile tugs at his lips.

"I was walking home, and it was dark. I decided to cut through the city park to save some time, and this fox just runs out in front of me from out of nowhere and stops right in my path. He stared up at me as though he was waiting for something."

"What did you do?"

He shrugs. "I thought he was a cute little guy and figured he was hungry or lost. I had some crackers in my pocket and offered them to him. He sniffed my hand, then arched his little fox brow, and told me: 'That's the best you can do?'"

"Oh, my gosh." I laugh. "What did you do?"

He shakes his head. "Well, naturally, I thought I was crazy at first. I was so convinced I'd lost it, I called Aris."

"Why Aris?"

"He's like a brother to me. I trust him with my life, and…" He grins. "Apparently, I trust him with my mental health as well."

"What did he say?"

"He told me about Fin, his… familiar."

My brows go up in surprise. "So, he already had Fin before you had Lynx?"

"No, he found Fin the same *night* I found Lynx."

My mouth drifts open. "That's incredible."

"We thought so too. I mean, it was already strange

enough we shared the same nightmare, but even more odd, we'd each get a familiar on the same night."

I think of Astra. "I wonder why I just found mine."

"I don't know," he says. "But there's one thing I do know."

"What's that?"

"Lynx, Astra, and Fin have a lot of explaining to do when we see them again. It seems they kept a lot of things to themselves."

"Well, according to Talina there's a reason they did that."

"But why? Wouldn't it be easier just to tell us?"

I shake my head. "I don't know."

With a heavy sigh, he lies back on his bed and stares up at the ceiling. "Even though I'm a bit irritated at Lynx for all the secrecy, I can't stay mad. It's strange to be without him; I miss him. I mean… he's become such a huge part of my life,"—his gaze darts to the foot of his bed—"I'm so used to Lynx being around all the time, you know? He's like family, like Aris and Fin."

I swallow against the sudden lump in my throat and lower my gaze. His words stir dark memories I'd rather not face tonight. His warm hand cups my chin, lifting my face back to meet his.

"I've said something that made you sad." Although he says this as a statement, I recognize it's also a question.

"It's all right," I reassure him. "Just memories."

"Of what?"

My bottom lip quivers, and I bite it softly to make it stop before I finally find my voice.

"My mom and sister."

"Did something happen to them?"

Emotions lodge in my throat, but I somehow manage to speak around them.

"They both died a few years ago. They were the only

family I had." An unbidden tear escapes my lashes, but I quickly brush it away.

"I'm so sorry, Kyra," he whispers. "My parents died when I was little. It's awful being alone. I'm sorry you lost them."

"Thank you. I rarely talk about them. It's…" My voice hitches.

"Painful," he finishes my sentence, and I nod. "But I've found it helps me a bit to speak of them," he adds.

I blink back tears as the memories flood my mind.

"I'm sorry about your parents too, Cael," I whisper as I take his hand, squeezing it gently. "How did you lose them?"

"A car accident when I was six years old." He sighs. "I don't have many memories of them, but the ones that I do… I know I was loved."

"My mom and my sister died the same way. We'd gone to celebrate my little sister's graduation and… on the way home there was a bad storm. Somehow my mom lost control of the car and we crashed." My voice quavers softly. "I was the only survivor."

He sits up and wraps his arms around me, running a hand soothingly up and down my back. "Oh, Kyra. I'm so sorry," he whispers. "That must have been terrible."

Unable to speak through my emotions, I nod.

When we finally pull away, he lies down and I do the same. He reaches his hand up and takes mine. With our fingers entwined, we lay there together. The silence between us is neither uncomfortable nor awkward because everything about Cael feels so familiar to me. As if I've known him my entire life.

A smile quirks my lips as more memories fill my mind. I remember when we first met in our last life. We were only seventeen. He'd been sent from Earth to train with our best knights so he could become my guard. He was so handsome as he stood before me, pledging his eternal fealty.

After a while, my eyelids blink open and closed as I struggle to stay awake. I look down at Cael once more, and he smiles up at me.

"Goodnight, Kyra."

"Goodnight, Cael."

CHAPTER 15

CAEL

She falls asleep, still holding my hand, and despite my discomfort from such an awkward position of holding up my arm, I'm reluctant to let go. I fight the urge to close my eyes, wanting to stay awake as long as possible. Even though I trust Willow and Talina, I haven't forgotten that Kyra and I are being hunted.

I know I should rest, but it's hard to still my mind. Myriad images float through my thoughts both of my previous life and of this one. In our old life, Kyra and I were lovers. I'm certain of it. Our relationship was forbidden. I do not know why it was so, I only know that it led to her death somehow. Surely that must be what Talina was trying to warn me about.

Closing my eyes, I vow that I will not make the same mistake again. I cannot deny that I am drawn to Kyra, but I cannot allow myself to fall in love with her. Not in this life. I will not let my feelings put her in danger like they did before.

Closing my eyes, I allow myself to drift away into sleep.

~

Sunlight filters in through the curtain, casting a soft orange glow through the room. I sit up and find Kyra still asleep in the bed, her blond hair spread out beneath her head like a beautiful halo. Long, blond lashes fan over soft pink cheeks and her lips are partially open in a small *o*. She is so lovely, she appears ethereal—angelic as she sleeps.

My fingers flex and extend with want to touch her, but I force myself to hold back. I am completely captivated as I stare down at her asleep in the bed.

As if knowing how much I long to study her luminous blue eyes, her eyelids flutter and open, and she gives me a sleepy smile.

"Good morning."

"Good morning. Are you hungry?"

She nods.

"I'll go find out what there is to eat. I'll be back shortly."

She stretches her arms over her head and rolls onto her side. My gaze travels over her lithe form a moment before I force myself to look away. No matter how much I want her, she cannot be mine. I am her guard and it is my job to protect her. That is all that matters.

When I step out into the living area, Willow and Talina are already awake, and the small table in the kitchen is set with two plates for me and Kyra.

Willow studies me with a piercing gaze as I approach.

"Talina said she sensed something when she took your hand."

I dart a glance at her daughter and nod. "Yes. We are supposed to find four guards."

The old woman lifts her upturned palm out to me. "May I read you?"

I don't see the harm. Besides, I'm desperate for answers

or any information that can help us. Cautiously, I take her hand.

She closes her eyes and bows her head. A subtle warmth travels across my palm as light glows softly around our joined hands. After a moment, she lifts her eyes to study mine in concern.

"The God of Creation granted your wish, but not in the way that you think."

I stare at her in confusion. "What do you mean?"

"The other four guards… they are connected to you. It is… strange…" she finally says, her voice trailing off as she stares at the opposite wall with a faraway look.

"How so?" I ask, anxious to understand.

"I am uncertain," she admits. "I only know that the two of you will recognize them when they find you. You will know them by touch."

Again, my thoughts turn to Aris. He has to be one of the four. Why else would he and I share the same nightmare? Why else would we both have familiars? It cannot be simply coincidence.

Kyra walks in, and the old woman smiles, releasing her grip on my hand.

"I am glad you are awake. We have prepared breakfast." She gestures to her daughter. "And this will help you on your travels."

Talina steps forward and places a small satchel on the table. She reaches inside and pulls out several items. "Here is a tarp and two blankets, some cheese and bread." I listen carefully as she lists off a few more items, including a knife. When she lifts a coin bag, she gives Kyra a pained look. "I'm sorry, it's all we have in the way of coin. It isn't much, but it should help you to at least have a place to sleep and—"

Kyra takes her hand and smiles warmly. Her eyes dart briefly to me, then back to Talina.

"It is more than we could have asked for. Thank you. We appreciate everything you have done for us."

Willow looks between us. "Be careful not to draw any attention to yourselves. There are dark mages of destruction and light mages of creation searching for you. The dark mages are clever, so it is best not to engage with anyone you do not have to. And the light mages... not all of them are trustworthy either, even if they work for the God of Creation."

Willow moves closer to me, and when her eyes meet mine, her voice whispers in my mind.

"Guard her well. Do not make the same mistakes you made in the last life. You cannot afford to fail your queen. The fate of two worlds depends upon her."

CHAPTER 16

CAEL

Willow's words shake me to my core. Images of my nightmare replay in my mind. Closing my eyes against the painful memories, I draw in a deep breath and then meet Willow's gaze evenly as I vow, "I will guard her with my life."

She gives me a firm nod as I turn to leave with Kyra.

I'm not happy about leaving. The cottage was a refuge. A place I felt safe in a world we know nothing about. Out here, we're on our own. And the worst part is, we have no idea who to trust.

The storm passed through last night, but several dark clouds still blanket the sky above us. Kyra and I pull our hoods up over our heads as a fine mist of rain continues to fall.

Willow's house sits on the outskirts of the city and to reach our destination, the map shows we have to go straight through it. I am loath to have contact with more people, but we don't have a choice.

The heavy rains last night made the surrounding area nearly impassable because of the thick mud, so for now, we must stick to the cobblestone roads of the city.

As we move through the markets, I notice as several eyes, men in particular, observe Kyra with lustful gazes. She is beautiful, I know. Even with her hood partially covering her face, it is easy to see how attractive she is beneath it.

Fierce possessiveness fills me as she moves closer to my side, instinctively seeking my protection. I glare back at the men, wanting them to understand in no uncertain terms that she is with me. If any of them dare try to touch her, I will end them.

We pass a tavern full of people. Loud, raucous music and voices drift out to the street from inside. A scantily clad woman eyes me with a lascivious grin.

"Would you like to come in?" she winks at me.

I shake my head and wrap a protective arm around Kyra as we continue on. That is not a place where we need to be noticed and certainly not one where we will stop, even with the sign that advertises rooms for the night.

It does make me think, though. Where will we sleep? After we go through the town, there isn't another for what looks like several kilometers. I can't be sure since the map is a hand-drawn rendering, but it appeared to be very far. At least, we have food, water, and clothing.

Willow and Talina gave us a tarp and two blankets, probably because they realized we'd be sleeping in the woods during our journey. I look to Kyra. I hate feeling so lost here. I worry about where we will sleep and how we will travel.

My memories are returning, but not as quickly as I'd like. I wish I remembered more about this world—Lunaria. It's strange how it feels both so familiar and yet still so foreign in the same measure. I'm supposed to guard Kyra, but I'm worried that my lack of knowledge of this place could potentially lead us into danger.

As we continue down the cobbled streets, I note several men on horses. Dressed in shining red and gold armor and deep red leather pants with black boots, these guys look like knights of some sort.

I eye their horses with envy. It would certainly make travel much easier, but as I think of the coin purse and Willow's apology about how little it contained, I doubt we have the kind of money needed to purchase one.

We're almost at the edge of town when one of the knights calls out to us.

"Halt!"

I turn to face him, automatically placing myself between them and Kyra.

"Be careful on the roads outside of town." His sharp gaze travels over me from head to toe. "There are rumors of bandits in the area. It may not be safe to take your wife through the woods."

Kyra stiffens beside me but says nothing. I dip my chin in a subtle nod.

"Thank you for the warning, but we are traveling to see my wife's mother. She is... dying, and we have no choice but to chance the journey."

"Safe travels, then," he says.

With that, he and his partner turn, heading back into the heart of the town. Kyra looks up at me once they're out of hearing range.

"What do you think?" She eyes the road. "Should we try to find another way?"

A great forest stretches out before us. The deep rich purple and green leaves of the various trees would be a beautiful sight if I weren't so worried about what may be hidden there now that the knights have warned us of danger.

I think on the map Willow and Talina showed us. This is the only road between this town and the next.

"We don't have a choice," I tell her. "We'll just have to hide anytime we hear someone approach."

Remembering the knife, I dig through the satchel Willow and her daughter gave us. As soon as I find it, I hold it out to Kyra.

"Here, take this and hide it beneath your cloak."

She takes it from me. "What about you?"

I smile because her concern is touching. Touching but unnecessary. She is the one who is more important. "Keep it. I'll be fine." I decide to lighten the mood. I give her a teasing grin as I flex my biceps exaggeratively. "Fear not, my queen. No one would dare pick a fight with your brave and dashingly handsome guard."

She laughs. "All right, my 'brave and dashingly handsome guard.'" She rolls her eyes as a grin quirks her lips. "Let's go."

KYRA

I tuck the knife in the belt beneath my robe and then look up at Cael.

"Aris and I are both in martial arts," he adds. "I'm actually pretty good if I do say so myself." He makes another show of flexing his rather impressive biceps, then waggles his eyebrows to tease me.

A soft puff of air escapes me as I laugh. "I hope so."

His jaw drops as he gives me a mock wounded expression. "You doubt me?"

"Of course not," I grin.

He arches a brow.

"I just… don't want anything to happen to you. That's all."

His expression softens as he looks at me. "I feel the same about you. I'll be fine, Kyra. I promise. I just… I'd feel better about you having the knife."

The way he looks at me, his teal eyes full of intensity, makes my entire body flush with warmth.

"Thanks."

The cobblestone road gives way to dirt and mud the farther we get from the town. The canopy of trees overhead is so thick, it blocks out most of the light from the sun. The darkness makes it seem much later than it actually is and also makes my heart rate quicken each time I hear a strange noise.

I know this is a forest, and there is bound to be plenty of wildlife, but this is a new world. We have no idea what kinds of animals lurk here, which makes me apprehensive—that and the warning the knights gave us before we left. The last thing we need is to be accosted by bandits and thieves. Aside from taking what little possessions we have, who knows what else they might do to us.

And then I remember the men who were searching for us in the woods when we first arrived in this world. What if they're somehow following us? Unable to stop myself, I cast a worried glance over my shoulder, half expecting them to be coming down the road behind us.

When I see nothing, I release the breath I hadn't realized I'd been holding, glad that we're still alone here.

I wish Willow and Talina had given me some pants instead of this dress. The hem, heavy with water and mud, slaps against my ankles with each step. But the only pants they had they gave to Cael. He's such a good guy. I'm pretty sure if I'd asked him to, he would have given me the pants and worn the dress instead just so I'd be more comfortable.

As if reading my thoughts, he looks at me. "As soon as we can, we need to find you some pants."

"You read my mind. I was just thinking the same thing."

He looks down at his muddy pants and shoes and then laughs softly. "It's good Lynx isn't here. I already know he'd be complaining about walking in the mud."

"But he's a fox. Doesn't he enjoy nature?"

A soft puff of air escapes him as his lips curl up in a wistful smile. "The last time I took him camping, he complained almost the entire time about how much he missed our soft bed and wanted a warm bath." He shakes his head. "We ended up coming home a few days early and the moment we returned, he made me promise that we would never do that again."

I laugh. "Oh my gosh. He sounds so dramatic."

He grins. "You have no idea."

"What about Aris's peacock familiar? What is he like?"

Cael rolls his eyes. "Let's just say he and Lynx could be brothers as far as their personalities go. I've never seen two more picky individuals in all my life. Aris definitely has his hands full with Fin."

"Do you think Aris is going to be worried about you?"

"I'm sure he's worried about both of us. He knows I took you to my apartment, and he has a key. So, when he comes looking for us and finds the door kicked in, I'm sure he'll hit the panic button right away." He looks down at his hands. "I just hope he's all right."

"Me, too." I turn to him. "You said he has the same nightmare you do, the one you and I share."

"Yeah. His dreams are the same as mine, but I don't understand why."

"That's what doesn't make sense, unless maybe he was a guard as well," I offer. "But that does not sound right either because you both dream of holding me... I mean, the queen," I correct, "When she's dying."

He looks down at the ground. "The thing is... Aris and I have been searching for answers for such a long time. We both thought it was strange to dream the same thing, but we had no way to find out what it meant, and neither Lynx nor Fin knew the answers." He purses his lips. "Unless they were holding back the truth all this time."

I place a hand on his forearm, drawing his attention back to me.

"Our memories are starting to return, Cael. I have a feeling we're going to find the answers to all of our questions here."

"I hope so," he says. "It would be great to finally understand why we share the same dream. To remember everything that happened when we were—"

He stills and grasps my forearm, stopping me abruptly.

I go silent, my every sense on high alert as he scans the road ahead.

"What is it?" I whisper.

"Someone is coming."

I listen a moment but hear nothing.

"How can you tell?"

He turns to me, brows furrowed deeply. "Can you not hear them talking?"

I shake my head. "No, but I trust you."

"We have to hide."

He guides me into the forest behind him, pushing aside the thick brush to clear a path. My long skirt gets caught, jerking me back.

"Cael," I squeeze his hand to draw his attention.

He turns to me, trying to pull it loose, but it won't budge.

"Your knife," he says. "Quickly."

I remove it from my belt and hand it to him. He cuts away at the fabric, setting me free. Urgently, he pulls me further into the woods and deeper into the thick foliage. It's only now I detect the faint sound of voices drifting toward us from down the road. Panic tightens my chest as they draw closer while Cael and I crouch down in the brush.

The ground is soft beneath us from the rain the day before. Despite this, I cannot seem to get comfortable, but I force myself to remain still anyway. The last thing I want to do is draw anyone's attention.

Sweat beads across my brow as we wait. I've never been more afraid.

As if sensing my fear, Cael hands me my knife. I palm the handle a moment to reassure myself that I have a decent weapon before I tuck it in my boot, trying to make as little noise or movement as possible.

My every sense is heightened as I scan the road, waiting to see who it is that approaches. Not that I'd be able to easily tell friend from foe, but I cannot tell from the voices how many of them there are. I only know that they are a group of men—at least more than two from the different sounds of their voices.

My pulse pounds in my ears as they come into view. It's three men on horseback, each of them as rough-looking as you'd expect potential bandits to appear.

Dressed in dark leather pants and tunics, with thick, heavy boots, these guys look really intimidating. Each of them carries a long sword on their belt and several smaller knives. Their heads are shaved, and as I watch them speak back and forth to one another, I note they each seem to be missing several teeth.

"That last lot had enough gold, we're set for a while. Aren't we, lads?" One of them smirks.

"Yeah." Another laughs. "Too bad, we couldn't have more fun with the lady. Don't know why she had to throw herself off that cliff. We're nothing if not gentle lovers, wouldn't you agree?" he adds with an evil grin.

My stomach twists in a violent knot, and bile burns its way up my throat as I listen to them talk about all the horrible things they did to her before she took her life. Cael tightens his arm around my shoulder, pulling me close, every muscle in his body growing more and more tense as they continue to speak.

One pulls his horse up short on the road before us.

"I have to stop a moment, fellas."

They stop, and he dismounts. I hold my breath as he moves in our direction, worried he's somehow spotted us. Instead, he walks to the bushes and unfastens his trousers. I avert my eyes, and a moment later, the sound of splashing water fills the silence as he urinates nearby.

I look up again after it stops and watch as he refastens his clothing. He turns back to his friends, then halts, his gaze zeroing in on the torn fabric of my skirt left behind on the bushes.

"Hey," he says to his friends. "Take a look at this."

To my great dismay, the other two dismount. They look at the piece of torn skirt and then lift their eyes to scan the forest.

"I think we might have some company," one of them says.

Another shrugs. "It could be old."

An evil grin forms on the third man's face. "It's worth investigating. Especially after how much fun we had with the last one."

I've never been much of a praying person, but right now, I'm sending several silent prayers to whoever may be listening for these guys to just get back on their horses and go away. I'm terrified after hearing them talk about what they did to the last woman they found. Although they didn't specifically mention the fate of her companions, I doubt they left anyone alive.

Cael holds me even tighter as my heart thunders in my chest. I don't want to be captured, and I certainly don't want to die today. I palm the knife handle sticking out of my boot and wait in silence as the men scan the forest.

CHAPTER 18

CAEL

The men search the woods, unknowingly moving closer to our position. It's only a matter of time before they spot us. As we kneel on the ground, I sweep my hands over the damp earth and grasp a large stone.

I look at Kyra and open my palm, showing her the rock. Worried blue eyes meet mine a moment before I toss it far and away from us. It lands with a loud thud, and the three men's heads whip toward it, in the direction opposite our location.

"Over there," one of them says, and they take off.

Kyra's eyes lock on mine, full of determination, as I lift my hand to begin a silent countdown.

1… 2….3.

We jump up from the bushes and break into a run, heading straight for the horses on the road. My heart hammers in my chest. If I can at least get her on one in time, she has a chance to get away.

"There they are!" one of the men calls out, but I dare not waste time looking back. We have to get out of here now.

Kyra's long dress catches again in the bushes, and I curse out loud as the men race toward us. They're on us so quickly, there is no time to escape. I jump in front of her, intercepting the first one. I kick out at him, but he spins away at the last second, avoiding the blow. When he tries to hit back, I do the same.

The other two skirt around me, and I hear Kyra cry out in alarm. Turning my head to dart a quick glance in her direction, pain explodes across my skull as something hits the side of my head. The world spins and tilts all around me before everything goes dark.

A terrified scream startles me awake. My eyes snap open to stare up at the thick canopy of trees as everything comes back into focus. The sound of a struggle nearby makes my heart thunder when I hear Kyra's voice.

"No!"

I lift my head, and the world spins before righting itself. Not far from where I lie, Kyra is on the ground. Two of the men are holding her down while the other looms above her. Her legs kick and flail wildly as she struggles to free herself.

She manages to pull one arm from their grasp. Grabbing the knife from her boot in one fluid motion she sinks it deep into the closest man's chest.

He cries out and then falls to the ground, dead.

Kyra scrambles to her feet, but one of the men rushes her. She stumbles backward. Hitting the back of her head on a tree, she crumples to the ground.

Blinding rage courses through me as I race toward the

man and barrel into his back, knocking him to the ground. The other one is on me in seconds.

I twist onto my back as red fills my vision. Raising my hands in front of me to push him back, fire jumps from my palms and races toward him. I watch in shock as the flames burst across his chest, knocking him back to the ground.

He writhes on the forest floor in pain; his terrified cries filling the air as I turn to the other one.

"No!" he raises his arms as if to shield himself. "Please! No!"

Focusing all of my rage on him, a ball of fire erupts from my palms, blasting him square in the chest. He bursts into flames like the other, screaming in agony.

I rush to Kyra, dropping to my knees beside her and lifting her into my arms.

"Kyra?"

Her eyelids flutter open and closed.

"Cael," she barely manages. "Are they gone?"

The sound of crackling flames behind me and the absence of any other sound tells me they're dead. I've never killed a man before. At least, not in this life. But as I glance back at their charred and burning bodies, I feel no guilt or regret for ending their lives. They would have killed us both if they could.

"Yes."

I lift my gaze to the road. I don't want to stay here and risk drawing any more attention to ourselves. I look back down at Kyra.

"I'm going to get us out of here. All right?"

She nods weakly. I clench my jaw as my gaze rakes over her form. Her clothes are torn, and her cheek is swollen and bruised from where they hit her. As I lift her into my arms, the fabric falls open even more, revealing the curve of her breast. I lay the fabric back in place to cover her as best I can and carry her toward the horses.

I'm lucky they're not startled by strangers as we move toward them. There are three of them—two chestnut and one white. I look down at her.

"If I lift you into the saddle, can you hold on?"

She nods. "I—I think so."

Carefully, I lift her up onto one of the horses.

"I'm going to check the packs for any supplies or money. All right?"

She looks at me. "We should take two of the horses."

She's right. For now, we'll both ride on one, but it would be good to have two for when she is better.

I move to the smallest of the three horses and remove the pack, placing it on the white one we won't be riding just yet. Then, I remove his saddle and harness to set him free.

Satisfied after I've secured everything firmly in place, I take the reins of the white horse's harness and tie them loosely to the saddle of the horse Kyra is on. Climbing into the saddle behind her, I wrap one hand around her waist. She relaxes back against my chest.

"All right. We're going to get as far away from here as we can, then find somewhere to sleep for the night."

"Let's go," she whispers. "Before someone else comes."

With a quick flick of the reigns, the horse moves forward, and we continue down the road. Kyra covers her face as best she can with her hood and I do the same, so we don't attract too much attention if we pass anyone else on the road. After all, we still don't know who might be looking for us.

Luckily, we pass no one as we make our way to the next city. It would seem the bandits probably cleared this road of anyone traveling since they came from this direction. I shudder as I think on what could have happened. I almost failed her. Anger moves through me at the thought she could have died because of me. I was foolish, allowing myself to be distracted, and it could have cost her everything.

The sun begins to sink low on the horizon as we ride. I don't want to stop, but when the darkness begins to descend, we don't have a choice. Only a thin sliver of moonlight ahead provides any light, and what little there is, is not enough to safely navigate the roads.

I guide the horses off the main path and deep into the forest. The sound of running water ahead catches my attention, and I move toward it. Although we have water in our pack, it would be good to have another source to draw from.

I brush the hair back from Kyra's face and lean forward to whisper in her ear. "We're going to stop here for the night."

She twists her neck just enough for her eyes to meet mine, and I don't miss the sharp hiss of pain that escapes her with the small movement. "Are you sure it's safe?"

"Yes." I scan the forest around us again as I listen carefully for any sounds to indicate there may be people close by. "We haven't passed anyone, and I don't hear anything unusual. I believe we're alone out here."

When we reach a relatively clear spot, I dismount, then help her to the ground. She's silent as I dig through our belongings, pulling out the tarp and tying it between two trees to give us shelter if it rains. I remove the blankets next and spread them over the ground for bedding. I'm glad when I find more blankets in the packs we took from the men, so I use those as well.

A few pairs of trousers and shirts are mixed in their belongings, and I dart a glance at her torn clothing. This may be a bit large, but it will have to do. When I'm finished, I turn back to her.

"Are you hungry?"

She lifts a haunted gaze to me. "There's water nearby. I'd like to bathe first."

I lead her in the direction of the sound of the water. The stream isn't far from our camp, and as I test the temperature, it's not warm, but not exactly cold either. Kyra looks to me.

"Can you please turn around?"

At first, I don't realize what she's talking about, but then it dawns on me. I nod and turn my back so she can undress and bathe. A small splash tells me she's entered the water. I train one ear toward the forest, listening for any sound of unwanted visitors and the other toward her in case she needs something. When I hear her coming out of the water, a broken sob escapes her.

Spinning, I find her on the ground. I rush forward and kneel down beside her.

"What's wrong?"

"Nothing," her voice quavers softly.

"Are you all right?"

She lifts a tear-filled gaze to me and softly shakes her head. "No," she barely whispers.

My gaze travels over her nude form. Several cuts and dark bruises mar her skin, and anger flares inside me anew at the abuse she endured at the hands of those men. I quickly drape my cloak around her and gather her in my arms. She nestles into my embrace as I run a hand soothingly across her shoulders.

"I'm so sorry, Kyra. It's all my fault."

"No, Cael." She shakes her head, then looks up at me. "You rescued me. You saved me before they..." Her voice hitches.

Her words fill me with guilt. If I hadn't let myself get distracted, she wouldn't have been hurt.

Her entire form begins trembling and I notice her hands are curled into fists at her side.

"Kyra, what is wrong?" I ask gently. "Please. Tell me."

She lifts her gaze to mine, clenching her jaw. "I'm weak, Cael."

"You're hurt, but you will heal, Kyra. You—"

"That's not what I mean," she snaps, her eyes full of anger. "I couldn't defend myself. If you hadn't saved me, I would be dead. How am I supposed to save two worlds if I cannot even save myself?"

I place my hands on her shoulders. "Kyra, you're being too hard on yourself."

"No, I'm not, Cael. I'm supposed to be strong, but I'm not." She meets my gaze evenly. "I need you to teach me how to fight."

"Kyra, I'm your guard. It's my job to protect you. You don't need—"

"Yes, I do." She grits her teeth in pain and stands to full height. Tilting her chin up, she stares down at me with an imperious look. "If you are my guard and I am your queen, then I command you to teach me."

My mouth drifts open as I stare up at her. Her eyes burning with determination.

In this moment, we are no longer Cael and Kyra. Memories flood my mind and we are once again Bryndon and Alora. I remember moments like this. When she was not only my greatest love, she was first and foremost my queen. I would live for her. Breathe for her. Fight for her. And die for her. She did not have to ask this of me, for I gave my life and all that I was freely to my queen.

Alora was as fierce as she was beautiful and in Kyra's eyes I see her again, standing before me just as she did in our last life. Memories of pledging my fealty to her fill my mind as I cross my arm over my chest and bow low before her. "Yes, my queen. If that is what you wish, then that is what I shall do."

She blinks several times and her expression softens. Her mouth drifts open slightly as she stares down at me. "I... I remember this," she whispers more to herself than to me. "I

asked you this before and you were reluctant to teach me…
And yet, you did anyway because I ordered you to."

Holding her gaze, I rise to my feet. "Yes."

She reaches out to cup my cheek, her blue eyes searching mine in concern. "Tell me, Cael. Did I ask too much of you in our past life? Was I… cruel to you back then?"

A smile tugs at my lips as I shake my head. "Never, Alora." Her name escapes my lips in barely a whisper. The memory of the first time it slipped from my tongue without the word queen attached to it, surfaces in my mind.

Her eyes brighten with tears, but she blinks them back. "Bryndon," she says softly. "I remember your name from… before."

Hope sparks in my chest as I think on the first time my name escaped her lips as a breathless whisper, the day she told me she loved me. "Tell me, Kyra. Do you remember anything else?"

She takes my hand and then pulls it to her chest, resting my open palm directly over her heart. "I remember this." She lowers her gaze and shakes her head. "But I—" she stops short and then steps back.

My arm remains outstretched in the space between us, hanging there a moment before I lower it again to my side.

She continues. "I don't know if these feelings are mine or if they are hers." Her brow furrows softly before she looks away. "I'm sorry, Cael."

"It's all right," I murmur. "I understand."

My fingers ache with want to touch her again, but I dare not. She does not want this. She does not remember that she loves me yet. I drop my gaze to the ground. Even if she does, I cannot love her. She cannot be mine. It would make her vulnerable again, and I refuse to fail her as I did before.

When we walk back to our camp, I offer her the clothing I found. "I found you some clothes." I dip my chin in a subtle bow and then turn away. "I'll keep watch nearby so you may sleep."

I start to leave, but she grips my forearm, stopping me abruptly. "Wait. Please."

Concerned, I blink down at her and kneel by her side, searching her blue eyes.

"What is it?"

"Stay here with me." She pauses and then clears her throat. "I don't think it's a good idea for us to be separated."

"As you wish," the words spill from my lips as they used to in our past life when I'd do as she asked of me. "I will stay with you."

"Thank you, Cael."

She does not need to thank me. Does she not know that each time she asked this of me—to remain by her side—it was everything I ever wanted? As her eyes meet mine, I realize this is still true. I remember loving her. I love her still. But she cannot be mine.

With a heavy sigh, I force myself to look away. "Are you hungry?"

She nods. I rifle through the bag and find the dried meat, cheese, and bread Willow and her daughter packed for us, handing it to Kyra.

A small huff of air escapes me as I grin. She is just as she was before. One of the pickiest eaters I'd ever known. Her nose scrunches up rather adorably as she sniffs at each item before taking a few careful bites. I'm satisfied that she's at least eating some of it. That's good enough for now. I hand her the waterskin next so she can drink.

While she does that, I make sure the horses are taken care of, removing the heavy packs from their backs and brushing them down. I glance back at Kyra.

"They need water. I'm going to have to take them to the stream."

She swallows thickly, then nods. "Be careful."

I hurry down to the water and allow the horses to take their fill while I train my ears to the surrounding forest, listening for any sign we might not be alone here. Horses are smart animals, and the fact they seem so unconcerned by our surroundings puts me a bit more at ease as well.

Once they're finished, I lead them back to our camp and secure them to a nearby tree so they can graze. I'll have to find them some proper grain soon. Perhaps when we reach another town, I can use the gold we found in one of the packs to purchase some feed for them.

I sit down next to Kyra to eat. The food is not good but it is not terrible either. As far as travel rations go, I've had worse. A wistful smile curls my lips at the memory of the freeze-dried meals I'd packed for myself and Lynx when we went on the camping trip that he hated. I miss his furry little face and his mischievous ways.

When I'm finished, Kyra changes into the clean clothing we'd found.

Her small brow furrows softly, as she looks down at herself. The clothes are obviously too large and I know she's probably wondering how this will work. But, luckily for her, I found a few items that will help.

"We can use this belt,"—I hold it up—"to cinch the pants around your waist. It's... better than your dress, at least, right?"

"Much better," she mumbles. "That dress almost got me raped and you killed because it caught on the bushes." She reaches out to take my hand, giving it a gentle squeeze. Tears fill her eyes, but she blinks them back. "I didn't thank you properly for saving me, Cael. If not for you, I would have been—"

I place a finger to her lips to silence her. I do not want her thinking on the terrible things that could have happened, so I decide to tease her instead. "Unless you plan on apologizing, you do not need to say anything."

She frowns. "Apologizing?"

I arch a teasing brow. "I seem to remember you questioning my abilities back at Willows. When you asked me if I knew anything about guarding." Crossing my arms over my chest, I tip my chin up as I look down my nose at her. "Well?"

"Well... what?"

A sly grin curves my mouth. "It's obvious that your doubts were unfounded and I'm... waiting for you to apologize to your 'brave and dashingly handsome guard.'"

She scoffs and then playfully slaps at my shoulder as she rolls her eyes. "I'm sorry I doubted your skills, my 'brave and dashingly handsome guard.'"

"Thank you," I grin, and then my expression turns serious. "Now, I need you to acknowledge that I did not act alone in saving us."

Her small brow furrows deeply. "What?"

I lean forward, holding her gaze intently as I take her hand. "You killed one of the men before I could even do anything. It was not just my actions that saved us, Kyra. You are not weak." Feeling bold, I address her as I would have in our other life. "You are my queen and you are strong. We both saved each other today."

She gently squeezes my hand as a smile crests her lips. "Thank you, Cael."

I nod. "I'll keep watch while you rest."

She looks up at me. "Right now, you don't hear anything out there that could be a threat?" She gestures to the surrounding forest.

I shake my head.

Her gaze drops to my hands. "How did you know how to... make fire like that?"

I lift my hand to my face and flex my fingers as I study my

palm. "I'm not sure how I did it. I only know I was enraged at those men and what they were doing to—" I stop myself short, not wanting to remind her of what could have happened. Instead, I continue. "It just… came to me."

Her brows go up. "It just came to you?"

"I can't explain it, and I'm not sure if I can repeat it." I try to force the flames to appear again, but to no avail. My shoulders sag in defeat. "I can't reproduce it right now for some reason."

She blinks several times. "Maybe the more your memories return, you'll discover how to… make fire again."

"I hope so. That was a very handy ability to have." I flex my biceps at her and then grin. "But for now, I'll have to rely on my impressive muscles to defend us because I am a 'brave and dashingly handsome guard,' feared throughout the entire realm."

She laughs and my mouth drifts open in mock offense. "Really, Kyra. You wound me," I tease.

She laughs even louder and I'm glad. I love seeing her smile.

After a moment her expression sobers. A tear slips down her cheek, but she quickly brushes it away.

"I'm sorry. I'm not normally this… fragile."

"You're not fragile, Kyra. You were attacked. It's only natural to be upset."

"Yeah, but according to Willow and Talina, I'm supposed to be some sort of reincarnated queen who can harness these amazing powers and somehow save this world and ours." She shakes her head in frustration. "How am I supposed to do all that if I can't even fight off a few bandits?"

I take her hand. "If it makes you feel any better, I'm supposed to be your guard and protector, and I…" I clench my jaw as guilt rushes through me. "I let myself get distracted, and knocked out. It's my fault you could have been killed and I—"

She puts a finger to my lips to silence me and presses her forehead to mine.

"You saved me. That's all that matters."

"We saved each other," I correct.

She nods softly and closes her eyes. "Yes, we did."

An image flashes through my mind—a memory of us sparring with each other in the woods. She kicked out at me. Knocking me off balance, she rushed forward and held a blade to my throat as she grinned down at me, pride shining in her eyes. "Do you yield?" she asked.

I laughed. "Only to you, my queen."

Kyra's eyes snap open to meet mine, and I know by her expression that she saw the same memory.

"You saw it too?" she whispers, astonishment lacing her tone.

I nod.

"We really were them, weren't we?"

"Yes, we were."

She lies back on the blankets and gestures for me to lie down beside her. She turns on her side to face me.

The smell of the surrounding forest is strong, earthy and damp, and the warm, soft mint of her breath fans across my face with the cool night breeze. My heart begins hammering in my chest. I remember being this close to her in our past life.

"Tell me everything you remember."

I'm reluctant to tell her everything. She has asked that we be open and honest with each other and I want to respect her wishes, but I'm not sure I am ready to admit to feelings that I had in the past and still have even now. I'm certain, even though we were guard and queen, we were lovers as well. Our love was forbidden and somehow… it led to her death.

Her blue eyes search mine as she takes my hand. "Please, Cael. Tell me."

"I…" I stop, not wanting to admit to her what I feel, but I also don't want to hold back. My feelings for her grow stronger with each passing moment. I do not know if it's because of this place or because of the way she's touching me, but I'm struggling to fight the urge to pull her to me and crush my lips to hers. Shaking my head softly, I force myself to focus as I meet her gaze.

"I remember enough to know we were more than just queen and guard to one another. And even though I cannot access the memories entirely, I know that this love was forbidden and it—" I stop, not wanting to tell her.

"What is it?" she presses.

I clench my jaw. "Somehow it led to your death."

Her brow furrows. "How?"

"I don't know." I pause. "I only know that I failed you and… you died because of me."

She cups my cheek. "You cannot blame yourself for something that happened then."

My eyes snap up to hers. "But if we are them: Bryndon and Alora… then how can I not?"

She moves closer to me. "Just because something happened in our past life, doesn't mean it will happen in this one. We are not the same exact people. I mean… yes, we are Bryndon and Alora, but we are also Cael and Kyra. We're shaped by the experiences we've had in this life as well. So that makes us different. We're not bound to repeat everything as it was just because we have been reborn."

My heart clenches because she's right. Just because we were together in one life doesn't mean we would be together in this one. Yet as I stare across at her, I want nothing more than to take her in my arms and hold her close. I long to kiss her lips and lose myself in her embrace as I did so very long ago. With a heavy sigh, I nod because despite how strongly I feel, I cannot ignore Willow and Talina's warnings. My love led to her death and I vow that I will not fail her in this life.

I lower my gaze from hers. "You're right. Just because we were them does not mean we are the same people now, nor that we would make the same mistakes."

She squeezes my hand. "I think we should rest so we can start early in the morning."

"I'll stay awake and keep watch for a while."

She nestles even closer to me. "Thank you, Cael."

When I finally allow myself to drift away into sleep, memories flash through my mind—images of our past life. She was mine, and I was hers, but our relationship was dangerous... forbidden. She was destined to marry five others to keep the peace within her kingdom. They were meant to serve as her loyal protectors.

All the queens before her had a harem for this reason. But not her. She wanted only me. And because I was the only one she chose, she died because I was unable to protect her on my own.

When I awaken, I allow my gaze to travel over her sleeping form. Tears sting my eyes but I blink them back. I remember it now. If not for me, she would have taken a harem as she was supposed to. She would not have died because she would have been protected as all the queens who had come before her.

But I did not want to share her with anyone, so I did not press her to take the others as her mates like I should have done to protect her.

I was selfish and it cost us everything.

CHAPTER 19

KYRA

L ying in Cael's arms, flashes of memory begin to surface in my mind. I remember being in his arms like this. I remember loving him, wanting only him and no one else. My advisors urged me to take a harem as the queens before me had, but I refused because I wanted only Cael, and I also knew that Cael did not want to share me.

He would not and he could not. It would have broken him if I had taken another, so I didn't.

I was not supposed to fall in love with my guard, but it happened when we were young.

Images and memories flit through my mind as I fall away into the dreamscape.

"Come back here!" my mother cries out.

Without turning, I race away from the castle and into the forest. I don't want to be queen. I do not want the responsibilities she has laid out for my life, nor the men she has brought before me —each of them staring up at me expectantly, ready to take my hand and become part of my harem.

I certainly do not want to bind myself to those five men when I know I only want one—one who will never want to share me with another.

"Bryndon!" I call out as soon as I reach the edge of the forest. "Where are you?"

I smile as he rushes toward me, relieved he waited all day in our secret place for me to appear. He crushes his lips to mine.

"Where were you?" he breathes between kisses. "I was afraid you wouldn't come."

I wrap my arms around him and pull him closer.

"Mother says I'm to marry five men. That I must take a harem like her."

He rips his mouth from mine, staring at me in shock.

"And what did you tell her?"

"I want only you, Bryndon." I shake my head softly as a tear slips down my cheek. "You and no other."

He smiles and presses his lips again to mine. Wrapping his arms around me, he rolls me beneath him as he kisses me with a passion that steals the very breath from my lungs.

"I love you, Alora," he whispers into my mouth. "I love you so much."

I reach up and cup his cheek. "Make love to me, Bryndon."

His mouth drifts open. "But... we are not bonded to one another yet."

"And we won't be, Bryndon, if I go back to the castle now." A tear slips down my cheek. "I'm to be bonded to them in the morning."

He clenches his jaw as he stares down at me, fire burning in his gaze. "No," he grinds out. "You are mine. They cannot have you."

"Then, take me Bryndon. Seal me to you. If we do this, Mother will have to agree to let us bond." I smile up at him. "It would bind our life force together; she cannot undo it."

With a heavy sigh, he drops his head to the curve of my neck and shoulder, groaning in frustration.

"I want you, Alora, but not like this. Not when you are forced to do something you aren't ready for, just so you will not have to—"

I place my hands on either side of his face and force his gaze to mine.

"No one is forcing me. I've wanted you for so long, Bryndon. I've dreamed of this so many times, my love." I cup my hand to the back of his neck and pull his lips down to mine. "I want you, Bryndon. You and no other."

"You and no other," he whispers against my lips.

My eyes snap open. I'm wrapped in Cael's arms. I lift my head and find him asleep. I don't know how we became tangled up in each other, but my heart hammers and my entire body flushes with warmth as he tightens his hold around me, pulling my form even closer to his.

"Are you all right?" he rasps, blinking sleepily at me.

"I'm fine. I was just… dreaming."

"Did you remember anything new?" he asks.

"No." The lie burns like acid on my tongue, but I do not want to share such an intimate dream. Especially since I do not know if these feelings I have for him are mine or are they just lingering memory from our lives before?

I give him a faint smile. "We should go back to sleep."

"I'll rest just for a bit." He grins. "I've always been a light sleeper. Wake me if you need anything."

I nod, but in truth, I won't wake him unless it's an emergency. The dark circles under his eyes tell me he's exhausted, and he needs some sleep.

As he closes his eyes, I lie awake, listening to the nocturnal sounds of the forest. It's cold, but I won't suggest we build a fire. I suspect Cael didn't make one for fear it might draw attention to us. I'd rather be a bit chilled than an easy target for more bandits.

Besides, I'm still wrapped up in his arms and I'd prefer to remain this way. Not just for warmth, but because being with him like this… it feels right and I'm reluctant to leave his embrace.

My dream replays in my mind—the memory of my life before this one. I study Cael. His white hair hangs down just over his eyes, and I carefully brush it back. Everything about him draws me in, but I'm so confused.

How can I love a man I just met? And how do I know he's the same man I remember from our past life? What if I'm different as well?

After all, wasn't I the one who just made a point of telling him we are not exactly them: Bryndon and Alora?

I shake my head to clear my thoughts. I don't remember enough of that life to know one way or the other. All I know is I have feelings for Cael—strong ones—I just need to figure out if they're really mine or if they belong to the person I once was.

His eyes are still closed in sleep, and I can't help myself. I snuggle against him, breathing deeply of his masculine scent —a strange mixture somewhere between forest and rain.

As I lie awake, I think of the map and how far away our destination seemed from where we first started. Our first day on our own, and we were already attacked. These guys weren't even dark mages. They were just regular bandits, trolling the roads and looking for victims.

I'm ashamed how easily they were able to subdue me. I managed to kill one of them, but if it weren't for Cael I would have been raped and killed. I curl my hands into fists at my side. If I'm going to survive here, I need to learn how to fight—and I need to learn fast.

Willow and Talina alluded to the idea I should be able to wield some sort of power. Cael discovered his in the heat of the fight, but I didn't. If I have any powers, I need to figure out how to tap into them—the sooner, the better. I hate the idea of running across more bad guys and feeling as helpless as I did today.

I look at Cael. He protected me, and I want to make sure I can protect him as well.

CHAPTER 20

KYRA

The early morning rays of the sun peek over the horizon, setting the forest alight with soft yellow and orange muted tones. Cael opens his eyes and gives me a sleepy smile. He reaches out as if to cup my cheek but pulls his hand away at the last second as if thinking better of it.

"How are you feeling?"

I'm completely mesmerized as his teal eyes stare deep into mine. I force my gaze away before I answer. "I'm just a bit sore, but it's not bad. What about you?"

He lifts his hand out before him, then closes his eyes. A small ball of flame hovers over his palm, and I stare at it in wonder.

A smile curves my lips. "How did you do that? I thought you weren't able to recreate it?"

"I dreamed about it last night." He grins. "It was as if I remembered a lot of things. How to do this," he curls his fingers into his palm, snuffing out the flame. He opens them again, and another ball of fire appears. "And how to fight as well."

I sigh heavily in frustration. "I wish I could remember things like that."

"I think it's this place," he says, giving me a pitying smile. "The fact we're here. I think… with time, we'll start regaining more of our memories and our abilities."

"I hope you're right, but in the meantime, I want you to teach me how to fight."

He looks down, his brows knitting together in deep contemplation. I half expect him to offer resistance to the idea, but he looks back up and meets my eyes evenly. "As you wish, my queen."

I give him a beaming smile.

After we eat breakfast, we take the horses down to the stream for water. He secures them to a nearby tree, then turns to face me.

"Have you had any training before?"

With a heavy sigh, I lift my gaze to the tree canopy, ashamed to admit this.

"I've actually studied martial arts before, but… when those guys came at me… I don't know what happened. It was like I—I froze up and forgot everything. All of my skills were just… gone."

"It's normal to react that way when you're faced with something terrifying." His eyes meet mine with a knowing look. "It could happen to anyone."

"I doubt that."

"It's true," he says. "Even soldiers trained for battle freeze up sometimes." He spreads his feet wide and then moves into a defensive position. "Show me what you can do."

Without hesitation, I rush toward him. He tries to dodge me, but I'm faster. I grip his forearm as he tries to spin away. I use his own momentum to push him forward, nearly causing him to lose his balance and fall over.

He turns to face me with a wide grin. "You're good."

I narrow my eyes. "I want to be better. I want to be able to use this if or when someone comes after us again."

"We'll practice, then," he tells me. "Morning and night. Sound good?"

"Sounds good," I agree.

CHAPTER 21

CAEL

She spreads her feet apart in a defensive stance and I do the same. We circle one another a moment before she rushes toward me. I barely duck in time to avoid her attack. She grins as I regain my footing and face her down, readying myself.

I had worried that her smaller size made her weak, but she uses it to her advantage, forcing my center of gravity to shift in a way that challenges everything I know.

She jumps, spinning and kicking out with her left foot. I barely miss taking a direct blow to the head. She is an excellent sparring opponent just as she was in our last life.

Horrified that she almost hit me, she stops, and I use her hesitation to rush toward her, taking her in a defensive hold, instantly immobilizing her.

She struggles against me as I band one arm around her waist, pinning her arms at her sides. With her back to my front, I wrap my other arm around her neck, gripping her jaw firmly with my hand to keep her still. I lean down and whisper against her ear. "Never let your guard down when facing an enemy."

Her blue eyes burn with defiance as she turns her head to look back up at me, gritting her teeth as she tries to break free. "I didn't want to hurt you."

"I'm fine," I state firmly. "Never feel sympathy for your enemy, Kyra. They will only use your kindness and mercy against you. Now. Concentrate. You can break this hold, but only if you focus."

She struggles even more, growling in frustration. "My *enemy*," she emphasizes the word, is my friend, and I did not want to hurt him."

Memories of our sparring sessions in our previous life surface in my mind. We ended many of these sessions tangled up in each other's arms. Desire burns through me like fire as I remember those moments between us.

Right now, I want nothing more than to bear her to the ground and make passionate love to her. I clench my jaw as frustration fills me. We cannot be together. Not like before. I refuse to put her life in jeopardy.

I force myself to release her and step away before I succumb to temptation.

She gives me a confused look. "Why did you let go? I thought I was supposed to break free on my own."

My nostrils flare as she moves toward me. I draw her delicate scent deep into my lungs. My desire for her is so great it threatens to overwhelm me. Although it is difficult, I force myself to push down my longing, reminding myself that her life hangs in the balance and I cannot compromise her in any way.

I meet her eyes evenly. "I am your friend and your guard, but you must treat me as if I am an enemy when we spar. I want you to be prepared for anything, Kyra. Your life may depend on it someday."

A smile tugs at her lips as she stares up at me through long lashes. "I know. But it's hard because I don't want to hurt you, Cael."

My heart clenches as her gaze holds mine. I long to pull her into my arms and vow that I will be her shield—her guard and her protector. That I will allow no harm to ever come to her. But I know this is something that cannot be promised by anyone. And because I care for her... I must help her to be prepared for any dangers that we may face. "You would only hurt me if you were harmed because you held back during our training. You must treat me as you would an enemy, Kyra. That is how we both must train."

Her blue eyes stare deep into mine. Unable to stop myself, I reach out and cup her cheek. "I would protect you from all danger if I could, but I might not always be able to. You need to be prepared for whatever may come for us. Somehow, I failed you in our last life and I vow that I will not make the same mistake again. Do you understand?"

She nods and then turns her back to me. "Take me in the defensive hold again. I think I can break free of it this time."

My chest fills with pride. She is as fierce and strong in this life as she was in our last. "As you wish, my queen."

CHAPTER 22

KYRA

As we make our way down the road, I'm thankful for the horses because my entire body aches from all our sparring practice this morning. But it's frustrating how my horse seems to keep wanting to go off the path and graze. I constantly have to guide him back to the road. The fifth time it happens, I huff out an exasperated breath.

Cael grins back at me. "Problems?"

I roll my eyes. "I think you should ask my horse. Why do you get the good one, and I get the stubborn one?"

My horse's head jerks up.

"Stubborn?" the word echoes in my mind. *"I'm not stubborn. I am just hungry."*

I go still, blinking several times as I look to Cael.

"Did you just say something?" I ask, even though I know his lips didn't move.

He frowns. "I didn't say anything."

"I did," the voice says again.

I look down at my horse, and he turns his head back just enough to look at me.

"You're… talking to me?"

"Yes," he answers.

"But how?"

"I don't know. I'm just a horse. How should I know these things?"

"Just a horse?" I ask incredulously.

"A hungry one at that," he adds, sarcasm lacing his tone.

I'm so taken aback, I laugh. I'm talking to a horse.

"Are you all right?" Cael arches a brow and gives me a worried look. He leans across and places the back of his hand to my forehead as if checking for fever. "Do you feel feverish?"

I shake my head. "I'm fine. I just…" I look down at my horse, who is still looking back at me. "I'm talking to the horse."

His jaw drops, but he quickly snaps it shut. "You're talking to the horse? But how?"

I shrug. "I—I don't understand it either, but I know he's hungry." My horse nods, and Cael stares at me as if I've suddenly grown two heads. "So, I think we should take a short break and let him eat."

"My companion is hungry, too," the horse adds.

"Oh," I reply and then look to Cael. "He says your horse is hungry as well."

Cael and I dismount and lead the horses off the road to allow them to graze. Cael remains silent as if uncertain what to say. I don't like the idea of him thinking I'm crazy, so I turn to him.

"You believe me, right?"

"Yes, I'm just… considering all the implications."

"What do you mean?"

"I mean… do all animals talk? And are you going to be

able to communicate with everyone who crosses our path? Or only some?"

A soft puff of air escapes my lips as I laugh. I throw my arms around his neck and press a soft kiss to his cheek. His face turns bright red when I pull back.

"What was that for?"

I give him a beaming smile. "I'm just so glad you believe me."

His gaze holds mine a moment before he replies, "I'll always believe you."

I study him a moment and then hug him again. I don't think even my best friend, Claire, would have believed me. He embraces me warmly in return.

"Thank you, Cael. I'm so glad it's you."

"What do you mean?" he asks, his voice warm in my ear.

Still holding him close, I pull back just enough to stare deep into his eyes.

"Of all the people I could have been sent here with... I'm glad it was you."

He drops his forehead to mine as he whispers, "Me, too."

Now that my horse knows I can hear him, he's actually very demanding, going on several tangents, complaining he hasn't had a good apple in days. Cael's horse, on the other hand, is just the opposite. She's very calm... thoughtful in a way, musing about the fields we pass and thinking to herself how wonderful it would be to do nothing but graze all day long at her leisure.

I feel sorry for them having to lug us around, and try to think of a way we could give them a break. Then the thought occurs to me. When we reach our destination, we can set them free. I would set them free now if we didn't need them. I feel selfish asking them to carry us so far.

"Do you have a name?" I ask my horse, only now realizing I have not even asked.

"It's Nox, and my partner is Halen."

"Nox, we have far to go and—"

"You wish to set us free," he says, cutting me off.

"Yes, but I—"

"You need our help," he continues. *"And we offer it freely. You are the one foretold, and it is an honor to aid you in your quest."*

His response stuns me, and it takes me a moment to respond.

"How do you know this?"

"We both felt it the moment our previous riders found you. Your inner light is strong, Kyra. I doubt there are many who would miss it."

"You're talking about other animals, right?"

"And people. That is why you must take great care who you trust. All who sense your power will seek to be near you. They cannot help themselves."

"Why?"

"They are drawn to it."

His words fill me with apprehension.

Cael watches us, and I know he only catches one side of the conversation but doesn't interrupt me to ask questions. My silence and the worried look I imagine must be on my face catch his attention, and he tips his head to the side to regard me.

"What did he say?"

"His name is Nox, and his partner's name is Halen."

Nox tenses. *"Why do you not tell him the rest of what I said?"*

I remain silent.

"Ah," he says, understanding slipping into his tone. *"You do not wish to worry him."*

"Yes," I reply.

"*You should not keep secrets from your mate,*" he gently chastises.

"He's not my—"

"*There is a connection between you—a threaded lifeforce bond. You are sealed to one another. Do you not feel it? It is strong. Almost as much as the light you bear.*"

I'm shocked he mentions the lifeforce bond, the one I remember from my dream—my past life.

"*Bonds forged in love are not easily broken. He is your mate and you are his.*"

I look at Cael to find him staring at me, his teal eyes searching mine.

"Everything all right?"

I nod.

"*Where are the rest?*" Nox asks.

"The... rest?"

"*Your harem. The ones who are meant to guard and protect you.*"

I recall the dream—the faces of the five men I was supposed to marry. I dart a glance to Cael. "I... don't think I want that."

"*Do not make the same mistakes you made in the last life. You needed them then and you will need them now.*"

"How do you know so much?" I ask, curious to understand.

"*Halen and I... our previous owners were Mages of the Light.*" He pauses. "*They were killed, searching for you both, by the bandits that you found us with.*"

I inhale sharply. "Why were they looking for us?"

"*They said you were the Chosen One—the queen who has been reborn to save our world from destruction. They wanted only to help you in any way that they could.*"

I'm still considering his words when he sighs heavily.

"I miss them. They were kind masters."

My gaze drifts to Cael. I share everything with him except for the part about the lifeforce bond. For some reason, I cannot make myself tell him about it because I still do not even understand it myself. Nox is right. I feel connected to Cael, but it's all so confusing.

Memories of my past life blur with this one and I'm not sure if these feelings are entirely my own or merely echoes of the past. I trust Cael, but I don't want to get caught up in this now. We still don't know what we're going to find when we reach the tomb and find the crown. Right now, we just need to focus on completing our task and finding a way home. And hopefully, Lynx and Astra will show up and help us figure all of this out.

CHAPTER 23

CAEL

The past few days, the air has been heavy with moisture. Dark gray clouds hang overhead as if promising rain, but it has yet to appear. I'm hoping it does not until we are well past this area. Judging by the storm we experienced back at Willow's house, I doubt our tarp would do much to keep us dry.

Farther ahead, the softly glowing light of the next town illuminates the landscape all around it. Surrounded by a tall wooden barrier, it appears almost like a fort. I wonder what they are trying to keep out.

The sun sinks low on the horizon, and I am hesitant to enter this new place tonight. Something about it feels ominous, but I do not know why. I trust my instincts however. They've never led me astray before and I doubt they will now. I turn back to Kyra. "I think we should camp in the forest tonight."

"Why?"

"Something... seems off about this place."

"All right." She nods. "I trust you. We'll find a good place to camp, then go through the town tomorrow." She looks to Nox and then pats his neck. "We'll get you some tomorrow. I promise."

I arch a brow, wondering what he's talked her into now. I'm glad she has discovered she can converse with animals, but it makes for awkward conversation sometimes since I do not know for sure if she's speaking to me or Nox and Halen.

"What are you promising him now?" I tease.

She has promised Nox lots of things on this journey— carrots, apples, grain, a fresh bed of hay to spend the night on something soft, freedom when we reach our destination. The list is actually becoming rather long. Nox is very demanding.

"I promised him grain tomorrow. He's tired of grass."

I smile and wink at Nox. "Grain you shall have, my friend." I gently pat Halen's neck. "And what about you?"

"She says grain will suffice for her as well," Kyra smiles.

We make our way into the woods. I train my ears both to the forest and the road behind us, listening for any sounds we are being followed, that we are not alone here. I notice nothing but the nocturnal noise of the animals that make their homes in the woods, but I still lead us farther into the thicket to hide our camp from prying eyes.

As soon as we dismount, a loud crack of thunder startles us both. Lifting my gaze to the sky, I watch as lightning arcs across the dark clouds. The heavens open up. Heavy rain pelts the earth in thick sheets. Nox and Halen's eyes are wide, and I know they are on edge.

"They can't stay out in this." Kyra gestures to the horses before she wraps her arms around her shivering form. "It's too cold for them. And for us," she adds through chattering teeth.

We make our way back to the road. The rains have turned the ground into slush. The thick mud makes it difficult for the horses to navigate, and I worry they will fall. Kyra and I dismount and lead them by their halters as we carefully pick our way through the sludge to the gates of the town.

As we draw closer, I marvel again at the wooden fort-like wall around the entire settlement. A wooden archway curves over the main entrance with the name of the town in big, bold letters: Orydon. Two massive wooden doors bar the entrance and I wonder at how many men it takes to open and close these mammoth structures.

I knock, and a piece of wood slides to the side in a small square cutout that's right near the level of my chin, revealing a pair of beady eyes.

"What business do you have here, stranger?" he grumbles.

"We need a place to shelter for the night… for us," I gesture to Kyra, "and our horses."

Despite the fact she's wearing a hooded cloak that shadows her face, his eyes widen as they alight on her. I do not like the way his lust-filled gaze travels up and down her form.

"Is there a place we may shelter?" I ask, drawing his attention back to me, my voice coming out more gruff than I'd intended.

"Aye. There is a place. The Queen's Inn. I'll tell you how to find it."

He closes the small opening, and a moment later, the doors begin to swing open. The large wooden structures groan as they are pulled back by four men, allowing us to enter.

All four of them eye Kyra as we pass. Fierce possessiveness fills me, and I wrap my arm around her waist, tugging her to my side. I do not want to leave any doubt in their minds she is with me, and I will protect her.

The first man points us in the direction of the inn, and we start on our way. The town has definitely seen better days.

Many of the wooden stores and houses are worn and rundown. Roofs of thatch are caved in or covered in tarps to keep out the rain in many places. Windows are broken or boarded up, and the cobbled streets are unkempt, several of the stones uprooted, broken, or missing. Trash litters either side of the street as if swept off the main thoroughfare in haste, but none of it cleaned up.

We pass a large tavern with raucous music. Several men and women stand near the entrance calling out to us as we pass, promising us all kinds of decadent enjoyments. Kyra instinctively moves closer to me when one of the men touches her arm and gives her a predatory look.

"I could give you a night to remember, beautiful lady. I promise you will enjoy it."

I step between her and the man, leveling a dark glare at him. "Touch her again and you die."

"All right." He puts his hands up in mock surrender. "My mistake. I didn't realize she was with you."

It doesn't take us long to get to the Queen's Inn. When we reach it, a woman is standing in the doorway, watching the rain.

"Are you looking for a room?" She grins, revealing a mouth missing several teeth.

"Yes," I reply, tugging Kyra even closer to me. "For me and my wife, and we need a stable for our two horses."

She nods, then looks over her shoulder, whistling to someone I cannot see. A man quickly runs out, and she tells him to show us the stables.

We follow him around the back, and I'm glad to see that the space has freshly laid hay, food, and water. The roof is thankfully intact, so everything is dry as well.

I arch a brow at Nox. "Does this meet your standards?"

He lifts his head in an approximation of a nod.

I remove the saddles, then take the satchels, pulling the

straps over my shoulders to carry them both. This place may look nice, but I don't want to leave all our belongings out here just in case. I toss a coin to the man.

"Will you see they are brushed down and taken care of?" I gesture to the horses.

His eyes go wide as he stares down at the coin. He lifts his gaze, blinking several times as if stunned by the amount I've given him. He bows low. "Of course, my Lord."

Panic fills me as I realize my mistake. I do not know what money is worth in this place, and I've obviously given him way more than the average person would. I only hope it doesn't make us a target in a place like this. Despite my worry, I force my face into an impassive mask and nod before we turn to leave.

Kyra's eyes meet mine, and it is easy to read the concern behind them. I'm sure she's thinking the same thing as me.

"We need to leave at first light," she whispers.

"Agreed."

When we enter the inn, I realize the first floor is a tavern. Several long wooden tables line the space, along with a few tucked in nooks and tables near the back. The woman who originally greeted us approaches and grins.

"The room comes with a meal." She gestures to the bubbling pot of soup hanging over the fire.

We sit down at one of the smaller tables near the back, and she brings us each a warm bowl of soup, a small loaf of bread. She starts to pour us some ale, but we insist upon water.

She tips her head to one side. "Are you on the path of the mage then?"

My brow furrows in confusion, but I say nothing.

Kyra answers slyly. "How could you tell?"

The woman laughs. "Only those studying to be mages, or who already are, refuse ale. They say it ruins their ability to cast or some such thing." She waves a dismissive hand. "Not worth the trouble if you ask me. Especially if you have to give up something as wonderful as the drink." She chuckles. "I'll be right back with your water."

I smile at Kyra. She's brilliant. That was an excellent way to gather information and will offer us some protection. From what I witnessed with Willow and Talina, a mage is probably rather powerful and not a person you'd want to mess with. I'll rest a little easier tonight.

We finish our meal in silence, each of us afraid to speak and reveal anything about ourselves. Several pairs of not so discreet eyes study us intently. We're strangers here, and I suspect this place does not get many visitors.

When we're finished, the innkeeper shows us to our room upstairs. It's tiny and only has one small bed, with a thin comforter and two small pillows, but at least it appears clean. I'm surprised there is also a worn wooden table and chair off to one side. The nearly full moon shines brightly through the window on the opposite wall, and two lanterns and several candles are lit on the side table.

"It's not much," the innkeeper says. "But I keep it clean and tidy for weary travelers such as yourselves. And—" she gestures to a room divider in the far corner, "I've already had hot water drawn for a bath."

When she leaves, I secure the door with the chair, taking the opportunity to try the barrier spell Talina showed me. I'm not sure if it's as strong as it should be, but when I notice the soft glowing light of the spell around the door, I'm satisfied I at least was able to cast it. It's better than nothing.

Kyra smiles at me. "Impressive."

I bow lightly. "Thank you."

She turns to the room divider. "Are you going to bathe?" she asks, a bit hesitantly.

"No." I lift my arm and sniff at my armpit. "I don't think I smell too bad. What do you think?"

At first, her mouth drifts open, but she laughs when she realizes I am teasing her. She playfully slaps at my chest.

"Well, you're definitely not sleeping with me until you bathe, Cael."

My heart hammers as her words conjure images of her wrapped up in my arms in the bed. I know she did not mean it that way, but I cannot help but fantasize that she did.

I long to hold her in my arms. I've regained more and more of my memories of our life before, which has left me with a desire so great, I can hardly contain it. I love her. I want her—more than anything I've ever wanted before. Every time we touch, my need for her grows even stronger. She was mine and I was hers: body, mind, heart and soul. And the truth is, that I still feel this way. I cannot help it.

But I also know that it can never be. Not in this life. I will not risk her safety as I did before. I was reckless then. Blinded by my jealousy, I was happy that she wanted only me. Instead of encouraging her to take a harem, I selfishly kept her all to myself and it cost her everything. I remember the day she told me about the five men waiting for her, chosen by her mother. Just the thought of those men daring to touch her stirred fierce possessiveness in me.

And now… knowing we must find four other guards to aid us in our quest, I feel the same dark jealous possession I felt before.

"You can go now, Cael." Her soft voice calls me back from my troubled thoughts. My eyes snap up to meet hers. She's dressed in only a threadbare shirt. It is obviously meant for a man, but the way it hangs loose on her body, exposing the delicate curve of her neck and shoulder, my mouth goes dry just looking at her.

I force myself to turn away and go to the tub to bathe.

When I'm done, I slip on a clean shirt and loose pants to sleep in. She's already in the bed. I look down at the floor, puzzled when I don't see a blanket and pillow there for me like I'd expected.

As if sensing my question, she smiles. "You can sleep up in the bed with me if you'd like."

I swallow thickly. Of course, I want this. I want her—desperately. Steeling myself, I walk toward the bed.

I lift the edge of the blanket and crawl in beside her. She turns to face me, then snuggles against my chest. We've done this before when we camped, but something about being in the same bed makes it feel different, more intimate. It calls forth memories of our past life, and I find it difficult to ignore the emotions brimming just beneath the surface.

I love her, and I want her. But she cannot be mine.

With a heavy sigh I close my eyes, feigning exhaustion that I no longer feel now that she is in my arms. "Goodnight, Kyra."

"Goodnight, Cael."

She places her hand on my chest, resting her palm directly over my heart. It's pounding and I'm sure she feels it, but she says nothing.

My nostrils flare as I draw her delicate scent deep into my lungs. She nestles close against me and my body responds. My length hard and painfully erect beneath the comforter. I open my eyes and stare down at the obvious tent in the fabric, praying she doesn't look down and see it as well. The last thing I want is to make her uncomfortable in any way.

Asleep, she pushes the blanket down from her shoulders, revealing the threadbare shirt covering her chest. In the dim candlelight, I'm able to see the soft mounds of her breasts beneath the fabric. Her nipples a dusty pink color against the rest of her pale, creamy skin. My mouth waters with want to taste her. To brush my tongue over the soft peak and feel it stiffen beneath my attentions as I remember from our past life together.

Many nights, I would crave her in the darkness as she slept. I would gently roll her onto her back and then move down her body. Parting her thighs, I would dip my head between them and slick my tongue between her soft folds, awakening her with pleasure.

I remember the way she used to run her fingers through my hair, guiding me to the small bundle of nerves at the apex that would always drive her mad with desire when I teased it with my tongue.

Drawing in a deep breath, I force myself to push these lust-filled thoughts from my mind. She is not mine and she can never be.

When morning comes, I force myself to remain still, not wanting to wake her. The sound of her breathing is soft and even, telling me she is still asleep.

I look down at her. With her hand on my chest and her head on my shoulder, she sleeps so trustingly in my arms that it nearly breaks me. She shivers slightly and I reach down and pull the blanket up over her shoulder, making sure to cover her completely. I brush the hair back from her face and then press a soft kiss to her forehead. "I will not fail you this time, Kyra," I whisper. "I promise."

Soft light filters in through the window as dawn approaches. I know I should wake her soon, but I also know she needs rest. I'm torn. I want to leave this place as soon as possible, but this is the first time since we left Willow's that we have had a relatively comfortable place to rest.

She stirs softly in my arms and then gives me a sleepy smile. "How long have you been awake?"

"Not long," I lie. In truth, I slept very little. I was afraid to allow myself to fall into a deep sleep and risk someone coming upon us while we were unconscious. Even though I cast the protective ward on our door, I know it is not as strong as one cast by an actual mage.

As we pack our belongings, a sudden knock at the door startles us both.

"Breakfast comes with the room." I recognize the innkeeper's voice. "It's ready downstairs for you."

I look to Kyra and we exchange a knowing glance. We will not be going downstairs. At least, not conventionally anyway.

We decide it is best to leave unannounced, so we place several gold coins on the bed for the innkeeper, then slip quietly out the window. I go first and then Kyra throws our belongings down to me.

When she sits on the windowsill and looks down at me, her eyes are wide with fear. "I—I don't think I can do it."

I lift my arms up to her. "I'll catch you, Kyra. I promise."

She draws in a deep and steeling breath and then exhales slowly through pursed lips as she carefully turns and then lowers herself until she is hanging from the ledge. "You're not going to drop me, right?" she calls out over her shoulder.

"Never. I'll let you squash me first." I chuckle. "I promise."

A nervous laugh escapes her. "All right. I'm trusting you."

"On three," I tell her.

"Okay."

1…

Raucous laughter, from the tavern below, startles her and she loses her grip, her arms and legs flailing as she falls back.

I move up under her. Her left arm swings wide, smacking me in the face as I catch her.

The world tilts and spins a moment as I stumble back.

The air is forced from my lungs as she lands on top of me, crushing my chest.

She scrambles off me and cups my face. Her worried blue eyes stare down at me. "Cael, are you all right? Oh my god, I didn't mean to squash you. I'm so sorry."

KYRA

He groans in pain as he sits up. A lopsided grin curls his mouth. "I'm fine."

"No, you're not."

He hisses and bands an arm across his chest as he stands. "You're right," he chuckles softly. "You squashed me really good."

"I didn't mean to. I'm so sorry."

He laughs and then sucks in a sharp breath. "It's all right. Really. I'm strong." He flexes his biceps as he straightens his back. "Aren't you impressed by your 'brave and dashingly handsome guard'?"

I roll my eyes at his attempt to tease me while he's injured, and purse my lips. "Very."

He winks at me. "Good."

When we reach the horses, I'm glad when I notice no one nearby. Nox's head whips toward me.

"I'm glad you are here. I do not trust these people. I heard them whispering about you carrying many coins."

I relay what he said to Cael, confirming we've made the right choice to leave quietly and quickly this morning.

We place the saddles on our horses and secure our satchels tightly to their packs as well, not wanting to risk losing anything in case we have to run. We cover our faces with our hoods and then carefully lead the horses away from the stables and out onto the road.

Several people eye us warily as we pass, but no one makes a move to stop us. We use several of the smaller roads in the city to make our way through instead of remaining on the main thoroughfare in case we're being followed.

Neither of us speak. Both of us are on high alert for any sign of danger. Every now and then Cael stops and I do too as he listens for any strange sounds as we walk down the mostly empty streets. It's still early enough that not everyone has left their homes for the day.

This works to our advantage, allowing us to move much quicker than we would otherwise.

When we near the edge of the city, Cael lifts me onto Nox's back and then takes his seat atop Halen as we approach the gates. Several guards are waiting there, and a chill steals through me. I want to be well rid of this place as soon as possible.

"Something is following us. I can feel its darkness," Nox says.

"Cael," I whisper. "We have to hurry. Nox says someone is following us."

"Not someone," Nox corrects. *"Some Thing."*

A frisson of fear moves down my spine.

Cael meets my eyes evenly. "We're almost there."

"Where are you going?" one of the guards calls out to us.

Cael and I both stop as he addresses the man. "My wife and I are traveling through."

The guard's eyes cut to me, narrowing slightly as they

rake over my form. He turns his attention back to Cael. "Where are you traveling to?"

Cael extends his closed fist toward the man and when he opens his hand a ball of flame hovers just above his palm. "We are mages. Let us through."

Several of the guards move back, some of them stumbling over each other in the process.

"Of—of course," the first one says, his eyes wide with fear. He yells to the others. "Open the gates! Now!"

Cael glances back at me and I nod.

As we pass through the gates, the guards watch us warily.

When we reach the edge of the forest, Nox and Halen break into a run.

They continue until we're far enough into the woods that we can no longer see the city.

Concealed deep in the woods, Cael turns to me with questioning eyes a moment before his gaze drops to Nox.

"Something evil was there," Nox says. *"We felt it. Something is tracking your light."*

His words fill me with fear.

"What is he saying?" Cael asks.

"Are you not going to tell him? Is this not something he should know?"

"I..." I start to make an excuse but stop. He's right. I need to tell Cael. With a heavy sigh, I pull up alongside him. "There's something I have to tell you."

"What is it?"

As I explain what Nox has told me about something tracking my light, Cael's face darkens with worry.

"We will stick to sleeping in the forests from now on." He frowns. "You should have told me, Kyra. It put you at risk staying at the inn. We cannot risk being around many people."

"I'm sorry," I tell him. "I just didn't want you to worry."

His brow furrows deeply. "I'm your guard. It's my job to protect you."

Guilt fills me as I lower my gaze. I asked him to be honest with me, but I haven't done the same for him.

"What else are you not telling me, Kyra?"

"Nox says he can sense a bond between us, Cael," I admit. "He says… we are bound together."

Cael's eyes meet mine evenly. "That day in the woods. The day we first—"

"Made love," I finish his sentence.

His mouth drifts open. "You remember then," his voice is barely a whisper.

I nod.

He looks to me a moment more as if waiting for me to say something else. Instead, I say nothing. I'm afraid to speak anymore on things that I'm not sure I understand. I have all these feelings for Cael, but I still cannot tell if they are truly mine or if they are just memories of what was.

He turns his gaze back toward the road. "We need to keep moving. If we're being tracked, we have to find some way to lose whoever is tracking us before nightfall."

Cael is silent as we continue on our journey. Every now and then we stop, as we did in the town, so he can listen for anyone approaching. But each time, he shakes his head, indicating that he hears nothing.

"Do you know what was tracking us?" I ask Nox.

"The magic of the dark mages takes many forms. I do not know what it was, I only know it means you harm."

"Are you going to tell me what he's saying? Or are you going to keep that to yourself as well?" Cael asks, staring at me accusingly.

I bristle at his sharp tone. "Why are you so upset?"

Drawing in a deep breath, he clenches his jaw. "How am I supposed to protect you if you keep things from me?"

"I didn't want to worry you."

He stares at me incredulously. "It's my job to be worried. I have to protect you, Kyra. I can't fail you like I—"

"You didn't fail me," I counter.

"Yes, I did," he snaps. "It's my fault you died and I'll be damned if I allow it to happen again." His gaze burns with sadness and anger as he stares down at me. "Do not keep me in the dark again, Kyra. I cannot—"

His voice catches and he lowers his gaze.

I reach for him, but he pulls away, refusing to look at me. "We have to keep going. We need to find somewhere safe for the night."

"All right," I agree and we continue down the road.

I don't understand why he carries so much guilt for what happened in the past. That was an entirely different life from this one. We cannot change what came before. We are different than we were then.

But he does not see it this way. And I do not know how to absolve him of the guilt he carries deep inside.

We continue on in silence. When we reach a fork in the road, Cael continues straight ahead, moving us through the thick brush of the forest instead of choosing a path. He looks back at me. "We will turn left further up. This way we are not easily tracked."

His idea is smart. The fresh hoofprints would have led our pursuers on the right path, but now, they'll have a harder time knowing where we went since we did not immediately turn either way.

When we finally turn left, Cael leads us deep into the woods. So far away from the road, I can no longer see it. Nor can I even tell which direction it might be.

We dismount and he immediately goes about setting up our tarp and blankets, while I tend the horses.

Nox looks to me. *"I believe your mate is upset."*

I sigh. "You sure have that right."

His eyes meet mine. *"He is only worried for your safety."*

I huff out a frustrated breath. "I know."

Cael calls out behind me. "I've made the shelter and fixed the bedding. Your food and drink are already there. I'm going to keep watch while you rest."

"Cael?"

His head whips toward me. "Yes?"

"I'm sorry. All right. I don't know what else to say."

"It's fine," he says defeatedly.

"Is it?"

A faint smile tugs at his lips. "Yes."

I gesture to the bedding. "Stay with me."

He shakes his head. "I'm going to keep watch for a while. I'll come to bed later."

Too tired to argue with him, I nod.

When I lie down, I'm so exhausted, it doesn't take me long to drift off to sleep.

I dream of people storming the castle, an angry mob intent upon murdering me and stealing my powers for the God of destruction. Cael takes my hand, pulling me behind him as he cuts through the crowd with his sword, desperate to get me away from the castle to safety. But there are so many people, and we are only two. It's impossible and I worry we are not going to make it.

An evil presence fills my mind. Fear wraps tight around my chest, and I feel as if I cannot breathe.

"You will die, Queen Kyra," it whispers in the darkness. *"You will not live to inherit your full power."*

My eyes snap open, and the nightmare fades away. The lingering hint of darkness stays with me, and my heart hammers in my chest.

I look over at Cael and find him asleep beside me on the blanket. I stare up at the sky as I take his hand in mine and send a quiet prayer to the God of Creation.

"If I am truly your Guardian, please protect him. Something evil comes for me, and I do not want him to die."

Tears sting my eyes and I cannot blink them back. Sitting up, I wipe at my cheeks to brush them away, sniffling softly.

"What's wrong?" Cael rasps, as he sits up beside me, placing a hand on my shoulder.

"Nothing," I lie.

He goes completely still and I realize he knows I'm not telling him the truth. I turn to face him. "I'm sorry. I just… it was a bad dream."

"What was it?"

Although it is dark, the moon casts just enough light that I can make his face out rather clearly. The worry is easily read in his expression, and it breaks me because I know it is not for himself, but for me.

A broken sob escapes my throat. "I dreamed that you were in danger. You were going to die because you wanted to save me, Cael. And I—I don't want to lose you."

He pulls me to his chest, running his hand soothingly down my back.

It all feels so familiar, being in his arms like this. Fresh tears fill my eyes and stream down my face as I remember my nightmare and how sad he was as I lay dying. "I don't want to lose you again, Cael. Not now that I've found you. You are my one true love, Bryndon. I cannot lose you."

CHAPTER 25

CAEL

A memory fills my mind. I remember meeting with her secretly in the woods. Holding her in my arms, I dropped my forehead to hers as I whispered, "We should not fall in love."

A tear slipped down her cheek. She pressed her lips to mine, and I was lost.

Kyra inhales sharply as the memory fades and when her eyes meet mine, I know she has seen it too. "I remember," she breathes. "You told me we should not fall in love."

She reaches up to cup my cheek. "But it was already too late. I was in love with you long before then, my love."

"Kyra," I breathe as I brush a stray tendril of hair back from her face, tucking it behind her ear.

Her blue eyes search mine.

She is so beautiful I cannot speak. Words escape me as my gaze travels over her face—the delicate features of her cheeks, nose, and brow. I trace my fingers down her face to the hollow at the base of her neck, feeling the fluttering pulse just beneath the skin.

This was my favorite spot, the one that always told me how much she desired me. Her rapid pulse giving her away each time I touched her or moved my body over hers.

"We cannot," I barely manage. "We shouldn't."

She leans in, so close there is barely any space between us. My heart hammers as her blue eyes stare deep into mine. Desire burns through me like fire. I want her more than I have ever wanted anything before. She is mine and I am hers.

Softly, she presses her lips to mine. They are warm and softer than I remember. She wraps her arms around me, pulling me close.

"I remember this, Cael," she breathes between kisses. "I remember us, my love."

Her words are my undoing. The last of my resolve crumbles around me. I trace my tongue gently along the seam of her lips, asking for entrance. She gasps lightly at the sensation and my tongue finds hers, curling around it as I deepen our kiss.

I trail my hand down her body to the gentle flare of her hips and down the soft skin of her thigh. Cupping the back of her knee, I pull her leg over my hip. She gasps as my hardened length presses against her center, and it is the most exquisite torture I have ever known. Only the thin barrier of our clothing separates our bodies from joining as one. I long to seal her to me again as we did in our last life.

"You are mine," I breathe into her mouth.

She pulls back just enough to stare deep into my eyes.

"Yours," she whispers. "Seal me to you, my love, as we did that day in the forest."

Unable to hold back, I roll her beneath me. She opens her thighs and I settle between them. I kiss her long and deep.

She softly bites my lower lip as I pull back just enough to stare down at her.

Her long hair is spread out on the blanket beneath her like a golden halo. Her eyes are heavy-lidded as she stares up at me. I reach down to lightly touch the tips of my fingers to her cheek. A pink bloom trails in their wake as I gaze down at her beautiful face. I trace my hand down her neck and gently part the robe that covers her, baring her naked form to me. She is so perfect, it steals the breath from my lungs.

"Tell me you are mine," I breathe.

"I'm yours," she whispers. "Only yours."

She cups the back of my neck and pulls my lips back down to hers in a searing kiss. I pull back just enough to press tender kisses along her jaw and down the elegant curve of her neck to her chest. I trace my tongue along the gentle slope of one breast, then close my mouth over the soft globe.

She gasps as I lave my tongue across the peak, turning it into a hard-beaded tip. Her hands run through my hair, gripping the strands between her fingers, and holding me in place.

"Cael," she breathes out my name as I move to the other breast and give it the same attention.

I skim my hand down her body and cup her mons. She inhales sharply as I dip my fingers between her soft folds, already slick with arousal. I long to taste her sweet nectar on my tongue. I move down her body and carefully part her thighs, guiding her legs over my shoulders and opening her to me.

"You are perfect, Kyra," I whisper, then lower my head to taste her. I run my tongue through her folds. When I reach the small bundle of nerves at the apex, she gasps and arches up against me.

I long to bury my length deep inside her and fill her with

my seed, binding her again to me in this life as we were bound in the other. But first, I want to give her pleasure.

I carefully insert one finger just inside her channel and am surprised by how tight she is. My cock is hard and painfully erect as I imagine sheathing myself deep in her channel.

She threads her fingers through my hair, and a low moan escapes her.

"Please, Cael," she whispers.

As I tease my tongue over the small bundle of nerves, her entire body lights up with pleasure. I band one hand over her hips to hold her in place as she writhes beneath me.

Her entire body goes taut a moment before she cries out my name, flooding my tongue with the sweet nectar of her release.

She tugs at my shoulders, and I move back up her body, crushing my lips to hers. Her warm, wet heat seeps through the thin fabric of my pants against my hardened length. I long to take her and bind her to me as we did before. I groan as she rolls her hips against mine.

"I want you, Cael. So much, but I..." she looks up at me and it is easy to read the hesitation in her eyes.

We may have made love many times in our last life, but it will be our first time in this one.

I clench my jaw as desire burns through me like fire. Panting heavily, I stare down at her and cup her cheek.

"We do not have to do anything you do not wish. We can wait."

She reaches between us, and when her hand moves over my length, a sharp hiss escapes me.

"But what about you?" she asks. "You're still—"

I shake my head softly. "I can wait, Kyra. I will wait for you."

She kisses me again, then gently pushes my shoulders so I

roll onto my back. She unfastens my tunic and runs her delicate fingers over the muscles of my abdomen, following with her tongue. She dips her fingers beneath the waistband of my pants and pushes them down my hips.

I look down just as she wraps her hand around my length. Her mouth drifts open when she realizes her fingers don't quite touch.

"You're bigger than I remembered," she whispers, more to herself than to me. I don't know if this is true because I cannot think beyond the feel of her soft touch as she gently strokes my length.

Liquid beads on the tip, and I gasp as she dips her head down, taking me in her mouth. The breath explodes from my lungs as she swipes her tongue across the top. She cannot take all of me in her mouth, so she begins a gentle suction as she strokes the rest of my length.

"Kyra," I pant, "Please. You have to stop, or I'm going to..."

She lifts her head. "I want you," she whispers.

I want her, but not like this. Something dark and primal stirs deep inside me. If I cannot fill her womb with my seed, I long to mark her as mine.

Barely holding on to the last of my control, I pull her back up my body. I crush my lips to hers. My length is a hard bar against her abdomen. I roll her beneath me, and she wraps her hand around my cock, stroking me. That is my undoing.

My cock pulses in her hand as my release erupts from my body, covering her abdomen. I run my hand over her, marking her with my essence. I capture her mouth in a claiming kiss. When I pull back, she stares up at me in wonder as she touches my face and then traces her fingers over my ears.

"Cael," she smiles. "You're—"

I gasp as the memories wash over and through me. In our

previous life, I was able to shift forms. I remember it now. It was not a complete changing of form, merely some attributes. I was able to take on many forms, but I had five in particular I favored—a fox, a peacock, a spider, a serpent, and a dragon—each lending me different abilities. Of all of them, I remember she loved the fox the most.

She smiles up at me as she traces over my now pointed ears.

"I remember," she whispers. "I remember this." She takes my hand and places it on her abdomen, now covered with my seed. "You always felt compelled to mark me when you were in this form."

"It is instinct." I lower my head to the curve of her neck and shoulder, inhaling deeply of our combined release. "The primal need to cover you with my scent, so all males nearby will know you are mine." I look down at her and cup her cheek. "Tell me you are mine and mine alone. I need to hear it."

"Yours," she breathes. "I'm only yours." She brushes the hair back from my brow. "I only want you, Cael. I do not want anyone else, my love."

I hug her tightly, practically crushing her against my chest as happiness floods my being at her words. Although I know it is selfish of me because a queen should always have a harem, I cannot share her. I simply can't. It would kill me to see her in the arms of another.

"Forgive me," I whisper, thinking about Willow's warning. She told me not to fail Kyra in this life as I did in the last. And the way I failed her was by depriving her of her harem with my jealousy. "Forgive me," I breathe against her skin. "I cannot bear to share you, my queen. I cannot."

She runs her hands up and down my back. The tips of her fingers trace delicate patterns along the length of my spine as she presses a soft kiss to my lips.

"I only want you, Cael. You and no other."

My heart clenches as she falls asleep in my embrace.

Guilt fills me as she lies so trustingly in my arms. I fear I am making the same mistake as before and I worry it will cost her everything as it did in our past life. I stare at the ceiling and send a quiet prayer to the God of Creation.

"Please," I beg him, "guide me." I wrap my arms even tighter around her. "I cannot lose her in this life. Not like I did before. I cannot bear it. Please. Tell me what to do."

There is no answer I can hear above the nocturnal sounds of the forest that surrounds us. If the God of Creation has heard me, he is silent. The mage said I made a bargain with him, but I do not remember the details. Part of me fears in asking Kyra to take no other mates, I've already broken our arrangement.

CHAPTER 26

KYRA

I wake in the morning with Cael's head between my thighs. He drags his tongue through my folds, and I gasp as he reaches the small bundle of nerves at the top. "Cael," I barely manage. My mind is telling me we should stop because we need to get on the road, but my body wants him so badly, it wins the argument. "Don't stop."

He grins, then continues to lave the small pearl of flesh that drives me mad with desire. He inserts one finger into my core, stroking in and out. I moan as I imagine it's his length filling my channel. I want him deep inside me, but I'm still a bit nervous.

He shifts back into his foxlike features, his ears becoming pointed as his beautiful white tail brushes against my leg.

When I come, it's with a keening cry. He moves quickly back up my body and kisses me deeply and passionately as he rolls his hips against mine. His length rests just to the left of where I want it so desperately to fill me.

I reach down and stroke him as he moves against me.

When he comes, he roars out my name as he paints my abdomen with his release. He smooths his hand up and down my body, covering me with his essence. He presses his lips to mine and breathes into my mouth.

"You are mine, Kyra. And I am yours."

I hug him to me as he collapses atop my body, pinning me beneath him on the blankets. I love the weight of him covering me like this.

"I want you and no other," I whisper into his ear. "I'm yours, and you're mine, Cael."

I lift my gaze to his. His eyes search mine as I reach up to touch his cheek. "Do you remember everything about us?" I whisper.

He closes his eyes and leans into my hand as if relishing my touch as he breathes out the words. "I remember our life together if that is what you are asking." He turns his head and presses a tender kiss to my palm.

Placing his hand over mine, he gives me a pained look. "I also know that my love for you put you in danger, Kyra."

I nod, because he is right. "You did not want me to take a harem. You couldn't stand the thought of anyone else touching me."

He clenches his jaw as he lowers his gaze. "I feel this way about the other four guards… even now," he admits. "Forgive me."

"There is nothing to forgive, Cael. It wasn't just you. I did not want anyone else either."

His eyes flick back up to meet mine. "And now? Do you still feel the same?"

"Yes, my love." I cup my hand to the back of his neck and pull his lips down to mine. "I only want you. You and no other."

CHAPTER 27

CAEL

It has been three long days and nights of hard travel, but we are almost there. Nox says he can still feel the magic of the dark mages pursuing us, but they are far enough behind that we do not have to worry. Yet.

The Capital city—Valyra—is just barely visible on the hill up ahead. The forest gives way to several acres of tilled fields, and despite the rich color of the earth, only a smattering of green crops dot the landscape, perhaps because the ground is so dry. We traverse a road so devoid of moisture, the horses kick up tufts of sand as we approach.

A tall castle sits directly in the center of the city—four white towers spiraling toward the clouds, capped with silver peaked rooftops—like a medieval fairy-tale castle.

When we reach the entrance to the city, the gates are open wide, and the dirt path gives way to cobbled streets. Although not in as much a state of disrepair as the last village, it is easy to see the structures and roads are not adequately maintained, and I wonder why.

"Willow said the Light Mage's Guild was located here, but I do not see it." Even as the words escape my mouth, my eyes scan the area and notice a large domed structure beside the castle that looks similar to an ancient cathedral but not quite.

Tall towers and spiers of white stone reach toward the sky. Large multicolored panes of glass line the windows in a brilliant display of color as the sun beats down from overhead. Silver capped rooftops glisten beneath the light and I stare at it in wonder.

Kyra points to it. "I think that must be it."

I nod. Willow told us to seek them out first before going to the castle or the ancient tomb. I am loath to be around more people, especially after what Nox told Kyra. I may not remember everything about this world, but I remember enough to know the inner light of the queen was one of the reasons she needed a harem. Many were drawn to her—some with good intent but many with that of evil.

Many wanted to steal her light and thus, her powers. The fastest way to do that was to murder her and absorb it as their own. That is why she had to be guarded and why I must guard her now. She is in danger from those who want to take her powers.

I think again about Lynx and Astra. Where are they? Why have they not come yet? I do not believe they are dead. Deep down, I feel as if I would know if something terrible had happened to Lynx. While I'm glad I do not feel this, I cannot help but worry.

As we make our way through the streets, several people stop and stare at us. Fierce protectiveness fills me, and I want only to take Kyra far away from all of this, but I cannot. We don't know how to get home, and even if we did, we'd be damning this world and ours if we do not complete our quest.

Remembering the terrible images of destruction that

Willow showed us, a small shudder runs through me. No. For better or worse, we must see this through. This is the reason we were reborn in this life. We have to save our two worlds.

When we reach the mage's guild, a man in long gray robes greets us as soon as we dismount. He motions for another man to watch Nox and Halen.

Kyra pats Nox on the nose, then says, "We will."

I can only assume he told her to be careful, which is what I would say if I were him.

She turns to me. "Nox says they want to stay here. This is where they came from with the light mages."

I look back at him and Halen and gently run my hand along his jaw. "Thank you, my friends. For all of your help."

Kyra smiles. "He says we will see them again."

I take her hand in mine as we face the light mage. He stares at us curiously. "You understand them?" he asks Kyra.

She nods.

A faint smile tips his lips as if satisfied by her answer. He bows low. "My queen. We have waited a long time for your arrival." He motions to the doors. "Come. We have much to tell you."

CHAPTER 28

CAEL

With Kyra's hand in mine, we follow behind the mage as he leads us into the building. Our footsteps echo as we walk beneath the massive domed ceiling. The entire structure is carved from white marbled stone with veins of black and gray. Intricate designs and patterns of nature scenes are etched into the stone, winding around the columns and up to the ceilings. Sunlight filters in through large stained-glass windows scattering a brilliant display of colors across the patterned tile floors.

Several mages, dressed in long gray and white robes, eye us curiously as we pass. Many dip their chins in a subtle bow to Kyra. If Nox's words are correct, they must recognize her light and who she is—the reincarnation of Queen Alora.

The mage leads us through a large set of doors into a huge library. Floor-to-ceiling walls of books and rolled scrolls and parchments stretch at least six stories high, each level with various ladders and walkways to reach them.

I notice a mage high up, returning a book and marvel at

how brave he is. I have always hated heights. Another mage walks toward us, this one wearing long white robes. She bows low as she approaches. Long black hair, streaked through with gray, hangs down around her shoulders. Her piercing lavender eyes study us from head to toe before she smiles warmly in greeting.

"I am High Mage Loryn, and I am honored to meet you both. We have been awaiting your return for many years."

Kyra meets her gaze evenly, looking every bit the queen I remember in our previous life. "It is good to see that the Light Mage's Guild still serve the God of Creation. But, I must ask… are they still loyal to their queen?"

Loryn bows low. "Of course, your majesty. That is why we have sent several mages to find you. The moment we sensed your return to this world."

I step forward. "Three of them were murdered on their journey."

Her mouth drifts open.

I continue. "We killed the men who took their lives."

She dips her chin in a subtle bow. "Then we thank you for avenging our brethren."

Kyra takes my hand. "We have come here for the crown. We also have many questions that we seek to answer."

The mage frowns as she cocks her head to the side to regard us. It doesn't escape my notice how her gaze lingers on our joined hands. "Then, you have been unable to access all of your memories?"

Kyra darts a glance at me. We anticipated this—the mages asking us questions that would reveal we have not regained all of our memories. But the light mages were always loyal to the queen. It is why the castle was built beside their citadel. Remembering the visions Willow showed us, we know we need answers and we need them now. We do not have time to allow our memories to return on their own. Not when the fate of two worlds hangs in the balance.

Kyra meets her eyes evenly. "Ever since we arrived here, we have been receiving random bits and fragments of our previous lives but not enough to... know exactly what happened in the past. How I died and what I must do here now."

"I will tell you all that I know," Loryn replies solemnly. Her gaze sweeps to me. "But it may be difficult to hear the truth of it."

Kyra narrows her eyes. "What do you mean?"

The light mage looks again to me.

"*He* was your downfall."

CAEL

"No," Kyra states firmly. "I don't believe that."

She defends me so vehemently, it tugs at my heart, but I fear the mage is right. I grit my teeth in frustration. As much as I dread it, I know we must hear the truth. If I am to make certain I do not repeat the mistakes I made in our past life, I need to know what happened.

"Please." I look to the mage. "Tell us everything you know."

She dips her head in a subtle bow.

"For that and for the crown, I must take you to the tomb."

We follow Loryn into a series of dark tunnels beneath the building. She conjures a sphere of light that hovers close to us as we walk, illuminating our path through the darkness. Fear coils tight around my spine. Although I have no memory of this place, my body instinctively reacts with a deep feeling of unease.

Each step fills me with dread. I do not want to continue, but I must know the truth. I need to understand exactly what happened so I can avoid the mistakes of the past. I cannot lose Kyra—not now. Not after we have found each other after all this time.

As if sensing my discomfort, she squeezes my hand as her blue eyes look up into mine.

"Whatever we find, Cael, it does not matter. I love you, and nothing will ever change that."

The mage's head turns back a bit and she slows her steps as if trying to listen to our conversation. There is something about her that has me on edge, so I make sure to keep my eyes trained on her at all times as we follow behind her.

We continue down a long, dark hallway, and flashes of memory begin to surface in my mind. I came this way many times after Alora's death. I remember it well. The guilt that consumed me was more than I could bear. The last time I came here, it was with a resolve to right things—no matter the cost to myself.

We reach a set of intricately carved metal doors. The finish, worn with age, reflects the glowing sphere as we approach. The mage raises her hand, and the doors open as if of their own accord, the groan of the hinges echoing eerily along the walls. She gestures for us to go inside, and for a moment, I cannot move.

I'm frozen in place as dread trickles down my spine. Kyra turns to me and stretches up on her toes. She wraps her arms around me, running her delicate fingers through the hair at the nape of my neck as she rests her forehead against mine.

"Whatever we find here, we are in this together. Nothing will change how I feel for you, Cael. You are mine. I want you and no other."

I notice the mage stiffen slightly at her words, but she says nothing.

We walk inside, and my eyes go to the large stone slab— the tomb of my beloved. My breath hitches in my throat, my entire body trembling as we approach. Emotions overwhelm me, and I fall to my knees before it as a tear slips down my cheek.

Kyra kneels beside me, wrapping her arm around my waist as she hugs me close.

"I lost you," my voice quavers. "It was my fault you died."

"What do you mean?"

Images fill my mind as the memories return.

"There was an ancient prophecy of the queen—the Chosen One. It said she would be murdered. She was destined to be slain by someone she loved."

"What are you talking about?" Kyra's eyes search mine.

Emotions lodge in my throat and I cannot speak around them.

The mage steps before us and continues, staring down at me with a look I cannot quite discern. "Because of the prophecy, the royal family dictated each queen would take a harem. They would not only help her to wield and control her powers, they would protect her at all times."

I reach out and gently touch Kyra's face. "But you refused to take any others because of me. Because I did not want to share you. I was selfish and—"

She shakes her head. "No, Cael. It was my decision, too. I remember that. It was my choice."

"It cost you your life, Kyra."

Her brow furrows softly. "I don't understand. How?"

The mage stares at me accusingly as she answers Kyra. "In his desperation to protect you from the prophecy, he made a deal with one of my brethren… or so he thought. It was a dark mage that deceived him—a follower of the God of Destruction."

She continues. "They poisoned his mind, and he turned against us. You were murdered by the very man you loved. If you'd had a harem, they would have protected you, but because you did not, the one who was supposed to be your sole protector is the one who was responsible for your death."

A deep ache settles in my chest as overwhelming pain and grief wash through me, and I feel as if I'm drowning.

Kyra gives me a pained look. "I don't believe it." Her head snaps toward the mage. "You're lying."

"Tell her." The mage gives me an icy glare. "Tell her the truth. I can see in your eyes that you remember."

I look down at my hands, remembering the blood that stained them that terrible night. "It's true," I barely manage. "I was placed under a spell. Dark mages stormed the castle. They attacked but I fought them back, slashing through them with my sword. We barely escaped; I was wounded in the process. We hid deep in the tunnels beneath the palace. But when we were alone, the dark mage I'd bargained with entered my mind."

I close my eyes against the pain, unable to look into the eyes of my beloved. "You begged me, Kyra. You pleaded with me not to harm you. But I was no longer in control." My voice breaks on the last word. "The moment it was done, I came back to myself, but it was too late. You died in my arms, trying to comfort me. Telling me it wasn't my fault, but it was."

"No, it wasn't," she protests. "It wasn't your fault. They poisoned your mind."

"Don't you understand?" I grip her shoulders firmly. "If I hadn't been jealous, you would have had a harem. You would have been protected. It was my selfishness that—"

"Stop! I don't care what you say. I will never blame you, Cael. I love you. Can't you see that? I always have."

The mage looks at Kyra in disbelief. "Even now, you would make excuses for the man responsible for your death? I will not allow history to repeat itself," she grits through her teeth. She raises her hands and I notice a flash of silver metal suspended between her palms. My eyes go wide as I realize it is a knife suspended by magic.

Her eyes are full of rage as she begins to speak words that I do not understand but know instinctively are part of her spell. She draws back and then sends the knife rushing toward me.

The world shifts into slow motion as the blade flies across the room. I know I will not be able to dodge it in time.

"No!" Kyra's voice rings out.

The knife stops midair, hovering directly in front of my chest. I blink several times in confusion, then look up at Kyra to find her hands out in front of her. Her expression is set in a mask of determination as sweat beads across her brow. Her entire body trembles as she struggles to hold it. Gritting her teeth, she cries out as she makes a slashing motion with her hands and the knife flies away, hitting the far wall with a metallic clang before dropping to the ground.

Fury burns in her eyes as she turns to the mage. "I am your Queen. How dare you try to take from me that which is mine?"

The mage's eyes are wide as she trembles, holding her hands out as if in surrender.

"Please." She drops to her knees and bows low. "I only did it to protect you. Can you not see history is repeating itself? I —I heard it with my own ears. You swore to him you would take no other mate, but you must. Can't you see? You have to."

"No," Kyra grinds out. "*I* choose who I love, and I want him and no other. Do *you* understand?"

"Yes," she nods shakily.

"I should kill you for what you just did."

The mage lifts her gaze with a hopeful look.

"Tell the others," Kyra says darkly. "I remember now who

I am, and I know my powers are greater than all of yours combined." Lifting her open palm, she conjures a ball of flame. "If you dare to harm Cael, I will raze this entire building to the ground and burn it to ash. Now, tell me. Where is the crown?"

Fire burns in her eyes as she speaks, giving her an other-worldly appearance. At this moment, she is the queen I remember—the all-powerful and mighty. The one who everyone feared and loved in equal measure.

The mage lifts a trembling arm and points toward the stone slab. "It is concealed by magic. Only the Chosen One can retrieve it."

Kyra turns a dark gaze to her. "How?"

"I—I do not know, my queen," the mage bows. "We have tried to retrieve it before but we could not."

I watch in awe as Kyra lifts her arms. Closing her eyes, she bows her head in concentration. Electricity sparks and crackles along the tips of her fingers a moment before a brilliant burst of light erupts from her palm and flies toward the slab, disappearing into the solid stone.

A ball of blue light emerges from the stone surface. I recognize the crown immediately as it floats suspended in the orb and floats toward us.

Kyra plucks it from the glowing sphere and places it on her head. Each stone of the setting is missing, but the intricately woven silver crown is just as beautiful as I remember.

Tilting her chin up, Kyra turns to the mage. "Now, go," she commands. "Leave before I change my mind."

"But, my queen, I—"

"I will summon you later," Kyra snaps. She looks at me. "We will go to the castle."

The mage blinks in shock. "The castle? But it has been sealed away by magic, and—"

Kyra levels an icy glare at her. "You think I cannot undo a simple spell?"

The mage's face pales and she says nothing. She quickly leaves.

Kyra turns to me and takes my hand.

"Let's go, my love. Let us go home."

CHAPTER 30

KYRA

Cael and I walk in silence as we make our way to the castle. The mages all bow before us as we pass, and I understand they do this as much out of respect for who I am as they do because they fear me. It was this way in the past as well. That is why they could not convince me to take a harem. They were afraid to anger me because they understood my power.

The image of the knife flying toward Cael replays in my mind. I almost lost him. I look down at my hands. I don't know how I summoned it, I only knew that I could. I called on the magic inside me to do my bidding and save Cael, and it worked.

Magic used to flow through my veins like a river, but now... I can sense only a mere echo of its former intensity, and I don't understand why.

The mages do not know this, however. I remember how they respected and deferred to my strength. I was the most powerful of any queen who had come before. Now, I want them to believe all my memories and power have returned to me, even though they have not. They must not know that I am not at full strength, or else they might make another attempt on Cael's life.

I must summon Astra and Lynx. I have to pull them across to this world. I don't know how, but I must. They are the only ones I know for sure that we can trust.

When we reach the palace gates, light shimmers softly around the entire structure. A barrier spell meant to seal the castle away not only from people but also from the ravages of time.

A smile curls my lips as I recognize the magic behind the spell. This was cast by my beloved Bryndon. I turn to Cael. He stares at the castle with his brow furrowed softly. "I did this. Didn't I?" he whispers.

I nod.

My gaze travels over the castle as memories flood my mind. Gleaming white towers spiral up toward the thin wisps of light-gray clouds. A vast mountain range capped with snow-white peaks spreads out behind it. The smooth walls of the palace reflect the sunlight with a pearlescent sheen with row upon row of large, open windows.

This place was built more for aesthetics than for defense. That is why we always cast a protective spell over the structure. Allowing only those who would do no harm to us, to pass through the invisible barrier.

As I raise my hands, I close my eyes and feel the magical force surrounding the castle. No one has entered this place since our deaths. Because Bryndon was my husband, he absorbed some of my powers. His magic was almost as strong as my own. None have been able to break through the barrier since it was cast.

I turn to Cael and take his hand in mine. This will take both of us.

Closing my eyes, I concentrate on unweaving the spell. I'm only vaguely aware of the people who have gathered behind us in the streets to witness this event, including several of the mages.

Sweat beads on my brow as I focus all my strength and power. I cannot fail. Not now and not in front of all these people. I must leave no doubt in their minds that I am as powerful as I was before. I cannot show weakness and risk anyone threatening our safety.

In the crowd, I hear whispers of doubt and disbelief among some of the people, but they do not matter. They will see I am who and what I claim.

Power flows from the tips of my fingers, extending to the spell surrounding the castle. Slowly, the fibers of magic begin to unwind as I concentrate on dissolving the barrier. It shimmers softly, then completely fades away. A collective gasp rises from the crowd as we step through the gates.

With Cael's hand in mine, we ascend the palace steps. The white marble and sparkling glass windows are immaculate after all these years, preserved by the enchantment. The front courtyard is filled with large trees full of heart-shaped purple leaves and thick, dark gray trunks and branches that twist up toward the sky. Various flowering plants with blooms of purples, blues and reds fill the entire space. The grass beneath is varying shades of lush green—the verdant shades richer than anything I've seen on Earth.

We follow a worn path with a small stream winding beside it. It is just as I remember. When we reach the large silver doors of the entrance, I stare in awe at the beautifully etched vines and flowers that cover them in a beautiful, woven pattern. I wave a hand, using my magic to open them.

Cael and I are silent as we step into the grand entryway. The ceiling is three stories tall, and the opposite wall is floor-to-ceiling windows that look out onto the gardens in the back. Two great staircases curve up along the wall to the second level and a balcony that overlooks the city and the mountains beyond the gardens.

A large statue stands in the center of the room, almost as tall as the ceiling. It is of me... as I was before I died—Queen Alora. It was a gift from a neighboring kingdom—a prince who sought my hand.

Wisps of memory float through my mind as Cael and I ascend the stairs. I trail my hand along the smoothly, polished wooden banister as I remember our life together here. It is both strange and familiar to return to this place. Everything is just as we left it... all those many long years ago.

It is a testament to the power of our combined magic that Cael was able to weave a spell strong enough to withstand the ravages of time and all the attempts I'm certain were made by the light mages to break it.

When we reach the top of the stairs, I look to Cael. Together, we raise our joined hands and create a protective barrier that will allow nothing and no one who means us harm to enter the palace.

I lead him to the bedroom... our bedroom. When we reach it, everything is as I remember it. My eyes sweep to the large four-poster bed. The deep gray wood is carved with a beautiful trailing pattern of vines and flowers. Bryndon had it made shortly after our bonding. The large white comforter with fine threads of silver woven throughout is just as soft as I recall. The massive fireplace directly opposite is still stacked with logs on the hearth.

The long silken white curtains wave gently as the cool night breeze drifts in through the open windows. I wave a hand to shut them and keep out the chilled air.

I remove the crown from my head and place it on the nightstand beside the bed. My gaze travels over the intertwining silver metal a moment before I look to Cael. "I remember there was a gemstone for each element. It helped me to wield the power of water, earth, wind, fire and spirit. But I do not know why they were removed from the crown and hidden. Do you have any memory of this?"

He shakes his head. "If I was the one who removed the gemstones after your... death, I do not remember it."

"Perhaps the memory will come later," I offer.

He sighs and then turns his attention to the fireplace. He opens his palm and conjures a flame to light the wood stacked on the hearth, warming the space. He turns to me, a smile tugging at his lips. "I hope so. I'm remembering more and more of our life here."

"I am too." My gaze drifts to the large rug on the floor near the fire. We made love there many times.

Cael walks toward me. His teal eyes meet mine full of desire. He's so close, the warmth of his body radiates to mine. He glances down at my lips and then back up to my eyes. I want him so much and I'm tired of waiting. "Make love to me, Cael."

I lean forward, ever so slightly but I pause as his breath catches in his throat.

"Are you sure?" he whispers. "Are you certain you want me?"

"More than anything," I breathe.

He remains still for a heartbeat and then threads his hand through my hair at the back of my neck. He grips the long strands between his fingers as he tips my face up to his. His eyes search mine for a moment before he captures my mouth in a claiming kiss.

Fire burns brightly within me, igniting the flame of my desire as his tongue finds mine and deepens our kiss.

"I need you," he breathes between kisses. "Tell me you are mine."

"I'm yours," I whisper.

He lifts me into his arms and takes me to the bed. He lays me down gently beneath the comforter, and then moves over me. He crushes his lips to mine in a searing kiss. I moan as he rolls his hips against me, and his hard length presses insistently to my core.

I reach down to cup him through the fabric of his pants, and he groans.

"Make love to me, Cael. I want to be sealed to you in this life as we were in the one before."

He stares down at me, his gaze full of fire and possession.

"You are certain?"

"Yes."

A shimmering light catches my eye in the corner, and I turn toward it. Cael does too.

"What is—" he starts, then stops when Lynx and Astra appear, seemingly out of thin air.

I smile at them, but Cael drops his head to my shoulder and groans low in frustration. He moves off of me and sits up to shoot Lynx an irritated look.

"Now you choose to show up?" He grumbles at the fox.

Lynx gives him a sly grin. "I take it you didn't miss me?"

Cael rolls his eyes. "That's not what I meant."

"Where were you?" I ask them. "We were worried about you both."

Astra looks to Lynx, and something unspoken passes between them.

"Forgive us," she says solemnly. "We had to wait until you were ready."

"Ready?" Cael asks. "What do you mean?"

"After we took care of the dark mages who came for you, we knew we had to give you time."

"Time for what?" I ask incredulously. "We had no idea what was going on or even where we were."

Astra arches a brow. "And if we had merely told you everything instead of letting your memories slowly return on their own, would you have believed us?"

I lower my gaze. She has a point. To be honest, I probably would have doubted most of it.

Lynx's eyes dart between me and Cael. "We apologize for the interruption of your activities but—"

"We must go," Astra finishes his sentence. "You both need to get dressed."

"Go? Where?" I ask.

"You have not retrieved the fire gemstone," she says. "Now that you have returned, the dark mages will be coming for you. You will need its power to defend yourself. We cannot afford to waste any time."

"But we only just got back here," I protest.

She gives me a pointed look. "You must trust me."

I look at Cael. "All right. Let's go."

CHAPTER 31

CAEL

Holding the crown in her hands, Kyra closes her eyes and concentrates her magic on locating the gemstones that are missing. Astra said each of the five stones controlled a different element, allowing the queen to harness and wield her powers to greater effect.

As we stand before a full-length mirror, our images ripple and distort; finally fading away to reveal a desert. With Kyra's hand in mine, we step through and find ourselves ankle-deep in red sand.

The sun burns brightly overhead and the air is warm and dry. Not even a hint of moisture is carried on the wind. Wisps of dust and mica sweep across the dunes, flowing through the canyons and around the large rock formations like water in a desert sea.

As my gaze sweeps over the stark and barren landscape, I notice it is full of varying shades of red, orange, yellow, even a bit of grayish-blue. Some might consider this place beautiful, but I can think only of the dangers. I worry about the lack of water and heat of the sun overhead.

I turn to Astra. "How far do we have to go?"

"Not far," she says. "Only two days travel at most."

My eyes drift over the sand once more before I glance at her. "Is there a reason the portal placed us so far from our destination?"

She sighs. "This is the best I could do. The gemstones are not meant to be easy to find. The magic that keeps them hidden is the same magic that prevents me from creating a portal to their exact location. This is the closest I could get us."

"Who hid the stones originally?" I ask.

Astra frowns. "I do not know. Or if I did... I do not remember."

Lynx steps forward. "I have no memory of it either. It is strange that neither of us knows this information, is it not?"

I nod.

I lift my gaze to the sun again, then look back at Astra.

"It will be a long two days."

"Yeah," Kyra adds.

"We can stop there for the night." Lynx points in the distance. A tiny island of trees, like an oasis amidst an ocean of sand, appears so far away, I wonder how long it will take to reach it.

Lynx scans the terrain and then looks to us. "We must remain on the rock at all times. We should never travel over the open desert sand."

"Why?" I ask.

"Because there are all manner of predators that hunt beneath the sands."

His words fill me with fear. What kind of creatures could do something like that? Even as I think it, I know I do not want to find out.

As we move through the canyons, the wind howls around the towering rock formations, creating an eerie sound in the otherwise silent terrain.

I study the area and notice a small network of caves nearby. If we have to camp for the night, I'd rather be in a more permanent sort of shelter than out in the open in an oasis. "Why not just stay here for the night?" I ask.

"Because there is no water," Astra answers.

I blink down at her, frustrated at myself for not being more prepared. Once I saw the desert in the mirror, I should have realized we would need supplies. Inwardly, I curse myself for not thinking of it before now. "I should have brought our waterskins," I mumble under my breath.

Astra shakes her head. "Not everything can come through the portals."

Her words suggest there may be several things that cannot be brought through and while I'm eager to know more about this world, she doesn't explain any further and I'm too tired to ask right now.

The relentless heat of the sun beats down upon us, leaving me physically drained. I can hardly wait to make it to our destination and rest for the night. But as I lift my gaze and scan the desert ahead, the oasis still looks so very far away. My muscles burn in protest with each step, but I force myself to continue.

I glance at Kyra and then gently squeeze her hand.

She turns and gives me a faint smile, but it is easy to read the fatigue in her expression.

"Does this place feel familiar to you at all?" I ask, curious to know if she remembers anything new.

Her small brow furrows softly. "I have some memory of

this place, but I… do not think it was always a desert as it is now."

She's right. Images rush through my mind like waves crashing against rock. "This place used to be green and full of life. But something happened to change it." I look down at the ground, trying hard to recall what happened here, but I cannot remember. When I lift my gaze back to Kyra, I notice her staring into the desert with a faraway look.

"Whatever it was," she begins. "I feel as if it has something to do with a castle. There is something there that…" her gaze sweeps over the vast expanse of barren land, "caused all of this."

The moment the words leave her mouth, dread settles like a heavy stone in my gut. There is an evil presence here. Something that feeds off of life—that took from the area all around it and made it into a desert wasteland.

Whatever it is, I am not eager to find it. But deep in my heart, I know it is somehow tied to the gemstone. I worry that when we find the stone, we'll find the evil that inhabits this place.

CHAPTER 32

KYRA

Cael and Lynx are bickering off to the side, and I laugh as the fox arches a condescending brow.

"I did not lie to you."

"You withheld the truth, so that's kind of the same thing, don't you think?" Cael counters.

Lynx rolls his eyes. "I could not tell you things you weren't ready for. You must understand that."

"Well, I know someone who's not going to get any bacon anytime soon."

Lynx's jaw drops. "You cannot mean that."

"I do."

Lynx gasps. "You wouldn't."

"Think again," Cael smirks.

"Fine." Lynx tips up his head. "I will simply ask Kyra. She is kind and will not treat me so cruelly as to deny me food."

"Oh, I'm not denying you food." Cael grins. "Just bacon."

Lynx turns to me, and I laugh before he even opens his

mouth. He's so cute with his white fur and mischievous blue eyes as he blinks up at me with a pitiful look.

"Don't worry," I tell him. "I'll give you bacon."

Cael's jaw drops, and I gesture at Lynx.

"How can you say no to that face?"

"And what about me?" Astra asks. "I love fish."

I smile. "Then, fish you will have."

"You're going to spoil them," Cael grumbles.

"How can she spoil us?" Lynx asks. "We are part of both of you, so, technically, you are caring for yourselves."

"Wait," Cael's brow furrows in confusion. "What do you mean when you say you are part of us?"

Lynx gives him a guilty grin. "Oh, about that… I was going to explain…"

"You're withholding something else?" Cael asks accusingly. "What now?"

"It's not like that," Lynx protests, then rolls his eyes. "Really, Cael, you wound me. I merely forgot to mention it. I was withholding nothing."

"What is it?" I ask.

Astra turns to me. "Since we are your familiars, you can join with us and increase your powers, including your ability to heal." She looks at Cael. "I would assume you have already discovered your ability to shift?"

I blink down at her. "How do you know that?"

She gives me a hesitant look. "We may have seen it when we were checking in on you both."

My jaw drops as I stare at her in shock. "You saw us…" I stop, unable to say the rest. I'm so embarrassed they were watching us when Cael shifted.

She nods. "Do not worry. It is nothing I have not seen before."

"That's an invasion of my privacy," I counter.

"I am your familiar, Kyra. I know everything about you, just as Lynx knows everything about Cael."

I'm not sure how I feel about this new information. I make a mental note to ask her more about it later when I'm not tired. Right now, I'm so exhausted, I can barely walk. I lift my head and notice we're almost to the oasis.

I glance at Cael. He looks just as worn out as I feel. "Are you all right?"

He nods. "I'll be fine." Lifting our joined hands to his face, he presses a tender kiss to the space between my thumb and forefinger and then gives me a faint smile. "At least we're together."

I squeeze his hand gently in return. "At least we're together," I agree.

CHAPTER 33

KYRA

When we reach the oasis, I'm surprised by how beautiful it is. Despite how exhausted I am, a cool drink of water from the nearby pool gives me a slight burst of energy and I'm eager to explore.

Tall trees with red and purple fanned leaves remind me of palm trees on earth but these are heavily laden with large, round pink fruit of some sort. A few of them lie scattered on the ground around the base of the trunks.

I pick one up and notice the flesh is tender; similar to a mango and it smells delicious. I look to Astra and Lynx. Are these safe to eat? When they nod, Cael and I peel back the outer flesh. No sooner do we create an opening, the entire outer layer seems to fold back on itself, pushing out the inner juicy meat.

The texture is similar to a mango but it's a deep purple color. I take a cautious bite. The sweet, citrusy flavor explodes across my tongue and before I can stop myself, I let out a small, appreciative moan. "This is wonderful."

Cael takes a bite and then closes his eyes as if relishing the taste. He smiles. "I remember these."

I study the fruit a moment and realize he's right. Memories flood my mind. "These only grew in the southern lands. The most fertile farmlands in all of Lunaria."

My gaze sweeps out across the desert and I turn to Lynx and Kyra. "What happened here?" I frown. "I feel as though I'm supposed to remember. As though... somehow I'm responsible for this in a way. Why is that?"

Astra steps forward. "You are right, Kyra. You are responsible for what happened here. You and Cael."

"What happened?" he asks.

Lynx sighs heavily. "Shortly before you became queen, a great evil spread through the land. Together, you were able to defeat it, but at great cost to those you love."

I blink down at them. "What do you mean? What cost?"

Astra places a paw on my forearm as she stares up at me with a saddened expression. "One of your fathers died here when he tried to defeat the evil that had come to this land."

"My... fathers?"

"One of the men in your mother's harem," she explains. "She had five mates; they all raised you as their own. But Jareth was the one you were closest to. He was the one who was killed when all of you fought to defeat the Great Serpent."

Memories rush toward me, crashing against my mind like waves upon rock. An image of Jareth's face surfaces in my thoughts and an unbidden tear slips down my cheek. "I remember him," my voice comes out barely a whisper. I lower my gaze to the sand. "I remember them all."

Sadness fills me so great, I can barely contain it. The loss of my mother and sister is the hardest thing I've ever dealt with in my life. But the memory of the loss of my mother and fathers in my previous life is just as unbearable.

Clenching my jaw, I fight back the tears that would come if I'd let them.

Cael wraps his arms around me, holding me close. "I'm sorry, Kyra. I remember them now too. They loved you. So much."

Despite my pain and sadness, I refuse to allow myself to wallow in grief. There will be time for that later. Right now, I have to focus. Curling my hands into fists at my side, anger fills me as I remember the evil serpent we trapped in the castle here so very long ago.

I turn to Astra. "It's been many years. The Great Serpent should be dead by now. Are you telling me it still lives?"

She nods. "I do not know how it is still alive, but it must be. The Great Serpent absorbs the life energy and power of everything nearby. That is the only thing that could explain why the lands around the castle are so barren even now."

"The castle," Cael begins. "That's where we're going, isn't it? The gemstone is there for some reason, but why?"

Lynx shakes his head. "I do not know." He darts a knowing glance at Astra. "But when the crown led us to this place, we suspected."

Cael looks to me. "You used the crown to find this place. Do you sense anything?"

As I gaze down at Astra, I narrow my eyes. "You said we're connected. You saw the same things that I did when I used the crown, didn't you?"

"Yes. That is how I know we are going in the right direction. I can feel the pull of the gemstone's power. The magic of the crown is drawn to it as well."

"I don't understand," I tell her. "Why have our memories not completely returned? How long will it take for them to come back?"

"According to everything foretold, you should have regained them all the moment you came back to this world,"

Lynx answers. "But for some reason, you are still missing pieces of your time here before."

"Then why don't you tell us?" Cael shoots him an irritated look. "I'm tired of being in the dark."

Lynx shakes his head. "You are supposed to be allowed to regain them on your own. Without our… interference."

I place my hands on my hips. "Who decided that?"

Astra meets my eyes evenly. "The God of Creation. The one whom you serve as his Guardians. Forgive me," she adds. "We would tell you everything if we could."

With a slight clench of my jaw, I nod and then turn away. I start back toward the edge of the water.

"Where are you going?" she calls after me.

"To bathe and then to sleep," I reply, trying but failing to suppress the bitter edge to my tone.

I understand why they are not telling us everything, but it still feels like a betrayal. Not just from her and Lynx but also from the God of Creation himself. Cael and I sacrificed so much in our previous life just to serve him and this is how he repays our loyalty?

I think on my father, Jareth. This is how the God that I serve repaid my father? He just stood by and allowed him to be killed by the Great Serpent when he could have easily offered his aid. Why didn't he?

In the back of my mind, I understand that there is a reason, but for the life of me I cannot remember what it is. And until my memories fully return, I never will.

Cael follows me silently and when I turn to face him, it is easy to read the frustration in his expression as well.

"I hate this," he says. "The not knowing. There is so much I still cannot recall and I feel like it's just there… out of reach."

"I know. I—" I stop abruptly as my gaze is drawn to a slight ripple in the water beside us. "Cael, did you see that?"

He frowns. "See what?"

I start to point, but a burst of water explodes from the surface.

A long rope-like appendage whips out and wraps tightly around Cael's leg.

His eyes go wide and he pushes me away to safety. I stumble back, falling onto the sand as the creature jerks him into the water.

"Run, Kyra!" he yells as he's pulled beneath the surface.

I scramble to my feet as Lynx and Astra rush toward us.

Astra jumps to me. Instinctively, I open my arms to catch her, and she disappears. Warmth fills my entire body as the familiar flare of magic floods my veins.

This is what I was missing when we were in the tomb. This is the power I remember—the magic coursing through me like fire and flame.

Anger churns deep inside me as I race toward the water. I will make this creature pay for daring to harm my mate. Power ripples through me as electricity sparks across the tips of my fingers. I raise my hands, directing my rage toward the water. A burst of energy erupts from my palms and races toward the surface, disappearing beneath the crystalline liquid.

The creature's body erupts from the water, suspended in the air. It releases a high-pitched screech as its rope-like arms hold tightly to Cael.

Its body is strange. With at least a dozen long whiplike tentacles and a large bulbous head with two beady eyes, its skin is clear to match the water. No wonder we didn't see it before.

Gritting my teeth, I direct all my focus to the terrifying creature, desperate to force it to release Cael from its deadly grasp.

Thoughts of intense blood and hunger fill my mind, and I

realize it is coming from the monster. *"Kill, kill, kill,"* the creature repeats in my mind like a dark chant of terror as it tightens its grip on Cael.

My beloved's eyes are wide with terror as they meet mine, fueling the fury that burns deep within me.

Power flows through my veins like liquid fire, leaving nothing but ash and devastation in its wake as I struggle to contain it, holding the creature suspended above the water. Barely able to hold onto it any longer, I cry out as I direct it toward the predator and jerk my hands apart.

The sick sound of ripping flesh fills the air as the monster tears in two and then goes still.

The tentacles fall away from Cael's body as it drops back to the water, sinking beneath the surface.

My hands shake as I hold Cael suspended in the air. Gathering the last of my strength, I carefully guide him to the shore and then lower him to the sand.

I drop to my knees beside him as he lies coughing and gasping. His entire body is covered in blood, with several small barbs sunk into his skin. He struggles to turn onto his side, groaning in pain.

Panicked, I look up at Lynx beside us. "What do we do?"

He moves to Cael's side and then disappears. I watch in wonder as Cael's body begins to glow softly.

"What's happening?" I reach for Astra with my thoughts.

Her voice fills my mind. *"Lynx has joined with him to heal him. He is a part of him, just as I am part of you. He is lending his magic to restore Cael's health. The barbs of that creature were poisonous."*

I watch in wonder as Cael's fox ears appear, along with his long white tail. Even in this form, he is handsome despite these odd features. Opening his eyes, they are a strange mixture of blue and teal. And I realize it is because he is joined with Lynx.

The barbs fall from his skin and I observe as the many wounds begin to close, stopping the bleeding.

I cup his cheek. "Are you all right?"

He smiles up at me. "Now, I am." His brow furrows softly. "It's strange, but now that I am joined with Lynx, all my senses are more heightened than they were before." His head snaps toward the desert, and his gaze sweeps across the sands.

His expression fills me with alarm. "What is it?"

"Something hunts us. A great evil has tracked us here."

The powerful magic coursing through me begins to fade as Astra appears beside me.

Cael levels an accusing glare at Astra. "You and Lynx both sensed this. Why did you not tell us?"

I watch as Cael's eyes return to their normal teal coloring as Lynx appears beside him. He lowers his head. "Because we must focus on moving forward, not on what is behind us. We cannot defeat this evil without the gemstone. It is too powerful."

Dread fills me. "How far away is it?"

Cael answers. "I was able to sense that it is far enough away that we can sleep tonight, but we must leave at first light."

KYRA

I'm exhausted and I don't know if it's from fighting the monster with the use of my magic or just the result of the long day of traveling. The sun has disappeared, taking the last of the day's warmth with it.

Now that his health is returning, Cael lifts his hands and creates a small flame in his palms, using it to light a fire to keep us warm. Lynx rejoined with him to complete his healing process even faster. Apparently, there was some sort of toxin in the barbs that had embedded in his skin, but Lynx assures us that his magic will heal Cael completely.

We sit around the fire, eating dried meat and cheese, along with a few of the delicious palm tree fruit. It isn't much, but I've learned to appreciate it with all the time spent traveling the roads.

"It's funny," he says, looking at me. "Now that Lynx has joined with me, I realize he was being honest. It makes me feel better to know he wasn't hiding things from me without reason. Even though I do not understand why, I saw his memory of the God of Creation instructing them that we need to learn the truth on our own."

His statement makes me wonder. When I was joined with Astra it felt like we were one, but I did not gain access to any new memories. I give her a questioning look. "What happens when you join with us? Are you still… you?"

She smiles. "In a way, yes."

Cael looks to me. "Lynx says it's difficult to explain."

I study his teal eyes now swirling with blue. "How long does he have to stay with you?"

He purses his lips. "He says all night to make certain I'm healed."

I understand what his expression means—no intimacy. At least… not the kind we were about to partake in before Lynx and Astra showed up.

Cael rolls his eyes.

"What is it?" I ask.

"Lynx says he's saving us from having cubs too early in our relationship."

I laugh as my cheeks heat in embarrassment.

Cael spreads a blanket on the sand for us to lie down. He lies next to me and wraps his arms around my form, tugging me against him. He curls his body protectively around mine, and I snuggle back against him. Despite how tired I am, I turn in his arms to face him. Reaching across, I brush the hair back from his face and cup his cheek.

"I love you, Cael. Whatever happens, I want you to remember that."

His brow furrows softly. "What's wrong?"

I lower my gaze. "Nothing."

Placing two fingers up under my chin, he tips my head up to face him. "Tell me, Kyra. Please."

I meet his eyes evenly. "When we reach the castle, I'm going in alone."

His head jerks back. "No. You need me."

I press my lips to his. "I know. That's why I can't lose you. I remember how horrible it was for my mother when she lost Jareth. I—" my voice catches. "I can't go through that. Not now that I've found you."

He drops his forehead to mine. "We're in this together, remember? You're not going in there alone. We're stronger when we combine our powers."

He's right, but I don't want to admit it. And I also don't want to spend tonight arguing either. So instead, I reluctantly nod, letting him think I agree even though I do not.

When we reach the castle, I'm going to have to find a way to keep him safe and away from danger. I'm going to face the Great Serpent alone and retrieve the gemstone myself. I cannot risk anything happening to Cael. I love him too much to lose him now.

He hugs me tight to his chest as he runs his fingers through my hair. "The mage... what she said about us repeating our mistakes... I—"

I place a finger to his lips to silence him.

"I only want you, Cael. You and no other."

With a slight clench of his jaw, he lowers his gaze.

"As much as it..." His breath hitches. "As hard as it is to even think of... I cannot allow my jealous and possessive nature to put you in danger, not like before. I could not bear it if something were to happen to you, Kyra."

I press a tender kiss to his lips. "I don't want anyone else."

"Lynx is in my head. He thinks..." Cael stops short as if what he means to say is too painful. "He thinks the other guards are supposed to be your mates as well."

"It doesn't matter. I only want you, Cael."

He grits his teeth. "I don't want you with anyone else either, Kyra, but I love you more than anything. I cannot allow my selfishness to put you in danger. Not again."

I press my finger again to his lips. "Do not speak of it anymore. I don't want to talk about it. I refuse to take anyone else. I refuse to have a harem when all I want is you, my love."

CHAPTER 35

CAEL

As she sleeps in my arms, Lynx whispers in my mind. He knows how strongly I feel for her, but he also knows the truth—she will not be safe unless she takes a harem. I cannot bear to lose her again, so I will have to find a way to live with it—to allow other men to touch her, to love her, and to seal her to them as I long to seal her to me as well.

The thought burns like poison in my mind, but I understand it has to be this way. Now, I will need to convince her before it's too late. As much as I want to, I cannot keep her all to myself. Her safety is more important than my jealous and possessive feelings. If I want to keep her alive, I must encourage her to take a harem as she should have before… and then, I will have to find a way to live with it.

"You are right to try to convince her of this. You do not want to repeat your mistakes of the past," Lynx whispers in my thoughts. *"I know it is hard for you to consider. But if you want to protect*

her, the cost is your heart. Are you willing to sacrifice for your queen? To share her with others as you were unable to before?"

Frustration burns through me, but I know he is right. *"I will do whatever it takes to keep Kyra alive. My vow."*

Closing my eyes, I try to get some sleep.

~

Something startles me awake, and my eyes snap open to the sound of distant voices. I gently shake Kyra's shoulder to wake her.

Her eyelids flutter and open. "What's wrong, Cael?"

"Someone is coming. We have to go. Now."

I look over at Astra curled up on the other side of Kyra. "Astra?"

Her blue eyes open and she instantly tenses. "Someone is coming," she whispers, and I nod.

Quietly, we slip into the darkness. With Lynx still joined to me, my night vision is acute, and I'm able to make out our path across the rocks and the desert sand.

My heart hammers as the voices grow louder, and I know Astra can hear them as well.

She looks to Kyra. "I'm going to join with you. We will be stronger together if we must fight." She jumps into Kyra's arms, then disappears. Kyra's blue eyes glow for a moment, then swirl with the green color of Astra's.

A loud boom behind me draws my attention, and I turn to see a ball of flame heading straight for us. Lightning fast, I grab Kyra and pull her out of the way, throwing myself over her and shielding her body as the fiery sphere crashes beside us.

"What is—" I start to ask, but Lynx whispers in my head.

"It is a Guardian of Destruction, and like you, he wields the element of fire."

I turn and conjure a ball of flame in my palms, concentrating my power and making it grow. My arms shake and electricity sparks across the tips of my fingers as I struggle to contain it.

Training all my senses toward the desert, I search for the location of the ones who mean us harm. Finding them, I push my hands out and send the fiery sphere flying toward our attackers.

The light arcs through the darkness as it flies out over the desert. My jaw drops as it illuminates our enemies. At least a dozen dark mages surround the Guardian of Destruction as he wields the power of fire in his hands, readying to attack us again.

"What do we do?" I ask Lynx.

"You must run! Until you have the gemstone, you cannot defeat them. There are too many."

Kyra turns to me. "I think I can—" she starts but stops, and I realize Astra must be speaking in her mind too. She looks at me, her eyes wide with panic. "Astra says we have to keep moving. We cannot defeat them without the gem. We need it to increase our powers."

CHAPTER 36

KYRA

As we race across the desert, Cael launches several fire attacks back at our pursuers, and they do the same. I can tell he's exhausted and I don't know how much longer he can keep it up. I want to help, but he and Astra and Lynx insist I must save my strength for when we reach the castle, where we will find the gemstone.

The Great Serpent awaits me there and I'll need all my powers to fight him and retrieve the magic stone.

A reflection catches my eye in the distance and I reach for Astra in my mind. *"Is that where we have to go?"*

"Yes," she replies. *"That is the castle."*

Cael stumbles as he throws back another flame, barely managing to catch himself before he falls. He turns to me and it is easy to read the exhaustion in his features. His gaze moves to the palace looming in the distance as he pants heavily. "We're almost there."

My heart hammers as I look to the castle. Its dark towers spiraling up toward the night sky like a sinister figure reaching for the moonlight above. Everything inside me screams that we should turn back, but I know we cannot. We don't have a choice. The gemstone is in there. I'm certain of it.

When we reach the front courtyard, I turn to Cael. I take his hand in my own and we lift our arms, summoning magic to create a protective barrier. Both of us are tired and I know the spell will not hold for long. We just need it to remain in place long enough to keep our attackers outside while we retrieve the gemstone within.

As the soft glow of the enchantment rises around us, sealing us in, a small shudder runs through me. Even though I know the spell does not work to trap us inside, I cannot help but feel that way anyhow as I turn my gaze back toward the darkened palace.

A cool breeze rushes across the sands, chilling me to my very bones as I look to the entrance.

The massive metal doors are open like a dark gaping maw, as if ready to swallow us the moment we step inside. I take Cael's hand in mine and squeeze it gently. "Stay here. Keep the mages and the dark Guardian away while I—"

He shakes his head. "You aren't going in there alone, Kyra."

He stares down at me with a determined gaze and I know there is no point in arguing this. The only thing I can do is go in first and hope that I can shield him if we're attacked.

Panic tightens my chest as another ball of flame races toward us, slamming into the barrier we've created around the castle.

We turn back toward the doors. With danger behind us and the unknown inside, our choices aren't many. We need the gemstone if we're going to make it out of here alive. Our powers alone are not strong enough without it.

Images of the destruction and ruin Willow showed us,

surface in my mind. Death and devastation await both this world and the one we came from if we do not stop the God of Destruction from having his way.

I look to Cael, and in his eyes I find the same resolve that I feel deep in my soul. This is why we were reborn. We are here because we have to save two worlds and we cannot fail in this quest.

CHAPTER 37

Still holding Cael's hand in my own, we step inside the entryway. Time slows and then stands still as a low buzzing hum fills my ears, followed by a sudden whoosh of air. The ground is ripped out from under me and I'm falling into darkness.

I slam against something solid and my eyes snap open to pitch-black nothingness. Terror stabs in my chest as I sweep out my arm and feel no one beside me.

"Cael!" I cry out, my voice echoing loudly all around me. "Cael!"

I close my eyes, trying to focus on Astra but realize she is no longer joined to me.

What happened? Where did everyone go? And where am I? Shaking my head, I struggle to focus but my mind is clouded in a thick shroud of fog.

I force myself to stand as I call out again.

No one answers. Wherever I am, I'm alone.

A thin sliver of moonlight filters in through the windows,

casting just enough light that I can make out a large shape in the distance. It begins to move toward me. My heart stops as I recognize the long sinuous movements. Dread trickles down my spine as a soft scraping sound of scales moving across stone fills the silence.

Glowing yellow eyes snap open in the darkness, casting just enough light to illuminate the sinister features of it's face. The Great Serpent flicks out his long, forked tongue as he stares at me with a predatory gaze.

He begins to circle me, his long body trailing behind him, creating a barrier between me and any chance of escape. "I'd heard the queen was coming to see me, but I did not believe you still lived." His voice is a low and sinister hiss in the darkness.

I still. Fear trickles down my spine as rough scales brush against my arm. I jerk it away.

"I have had many long years to think on my revenge."

I raise my hands up before me, readying to conjure whatever magic I can as his body begins coiling closer around me, the sound akin to the rough grating of sandpaper against stone.

"Where are my friends? Where am I? What do you want?"

A sudden rush of air whips around me and I gasp as he places his head directly before me. So close, the heat of his breath skates across my skin. He flicks out his tongue as if scenting the air. "I can scent your fear, my queen," he hisses.

The glowing light of his eyes is mesmerizing as I stare at his hooded cobra-like face.

Ice fills my veins as he bares his fangs, each of them at least as long as my forearm and dripping with venom. "You already know where you are, my queen." I note the condescension in its tone. "You are the one who trapped me here. Do you not remember?"

"Trapped you?" I blink several times in confusion. "What are you talking about?"

His glowing yellow eyes burn with anger. His long sinuous body coils even tighter around me, writhing as it undulates and moves over the floor.

He leans in, his vertically slit pupils contract and expand as he studies me intently.

"Oh, you don't remember, do you?" He cocks his head slightly to the side. "How odd."

"I—I don't understand."

"Then, let me help you."

Without warning, he strikes. Sharp fangs clamp down on my arm. I choke on a scream as they sink deep into my flesh. My vision begins to swim, and I fall back onto a solid wall of muscle. It moves beneath me, his tail coiling tight around my form as he lifts me into the air, my entire body limp.

Glowing yellow eyes stare deep into mine with a hypnotic gaze, and I stare transfixed, unable to look away. Images and wisps of memory fill my mind as I realize it is the serpent somehow accessing my thoughts, searching for something but I do not know what.

A dark and sinister chuckle rises from his throat. "Oh, now, I see. It all makes sense."

"What does?" I barely manage, struggling to keep my eyes open, even as the dark void beckons me.

"Let us check with your beloved, shall we?"

Its tail tightens around me and it starts toward the door. Soft light from the silver moon filters in through a long hallway of windows, casting just enough illumination that I can see our reflection along the mirrors lining the corridor.

An iridescent red shimmer glints off the shiny, inter-locking scales as the serpent's long sinuous body moves along the floor of the castle. Through the haze of the toxin coursing through my system my mind registers it as both terrifyingly beautiful and completely mesmerizing.

We enter a large room. Two large and elaborate chairs along the opposite wall tell me this must have been the throne room in a time long ago. On the floor in the center, Cael, Lynx, and Astra lie still and unmoving.

Alarm bursts through me. "Are they—"

I start to ask if they're dead, but the serpent replies, "Not yet. Your friends still live because I have many questions." He turns a sharp gaze to me. "Starting with… how can I free myself of this wretched prison you've kept me in all of these years?"

I know Astra said I fought him, but other than the death of my father, I do not remember any of the details. I certainly do not remember trapping him in the castle. "I don't know what you're talking about," I grind out. "You have the wrong person. I didn't put you here."

"Yessss," it hisses. "You did. It was my punishment for killing a human."

An image of Jareth surfaces in my mind and a tear slips down my cheek. Anger fills me as I meet his eyes evenly. "That human was my father," I grit through my teeth.

"If you want your friends to live, you will free me. Else, I have no use for you."

The memory of Jareth's body, torn and bloodied fills my thoughts as I glance at Cael. "Please." A tear slips down my cheek as I rack my brain. "You have to believe me. I don't remember doing this to you. If I did, I would help you go free so I could save them. I swear it."

"Let me check with your lover then. Perhaps he remembers more than you. After all, he was with you when you imprisoned me."

Lightning fast, I watch in horror as he strikes out and bites Cael.

Cael cries out. His eyes snap open and he looks up at the creature in terror. "What are you?" he slurs. His gaze sweeps to me, and panic twists his features. "Let her go!"

Instead of answering him, the serpent stares deep into his eyes. Cael goes silent, transfixed as I was by the creature's hypnotic gaze.

Another dark chuckle escapes it. "Oh, this is too good."

"What?" I ask.

It cocks its head to the side, regarding Cael with a sinister look.

"You prayed to the God of Creation after your beloved queen died by your hand, and he granted your request."

"What request?" Cael asks, echoing my own thoughts.

"It is the reason you do not remember trapping me here." It turns to me. "The reason not all of your memories have returned."

I shake my head. "You're not making sense. What are you talking about?"

"Your guard blamed himself for your death. Because of him, you did not take a harem as every queen before you had done for her own protection. He mourned at your tomb and called upon the God of Creation, begging him to restore your life. To his surprise, the god answered."

"What happened?" I ask, desperate to understand.

He turns his attention back to Cael. "The god told you she would be reborn… you both would. So, you begged him to force her to accept the harem she should have chosen before. You wanted to make sure you did not repeat your mistake. You wanted to make sure she did not choose *only* you to protect her, leaving her vulnerable again in the next life." It tips its head to the side as if studying Cael intently. "The god granted your request, but not in the way you thought he would."

"What do you mean?"

An evil grin lights his face. "You were destined to take five mates in this life, according to the prayer he'd been granted. But that was before you found me. Now, you will die before any of that happens."

"Wait!" I cry out, stalling for time but also desperate to know the answer. "What do you mean the god granted his request but not in the way that he thought?"

The Great Serpent turns his attention back to me, ignoring Cael behind him. His long tail snakes around my form, tightening to the point that I can barely breathe.

Cael lifts his open palms and creates a ball of flame. Standing behind the serpent, his eyes meet mine, and I know what he means to do.

"Please. Answer me before you kill me," I address the serpent, trying to keep his focus on me.

I shudder inwardly, as his long, forked tongue flicks out and licks across my skin. He tips his head to the side as if considering.

"Why should I tell you?" he asks. "I should just crush your pitiful form and be done with it."

Panic tightens my chest as I force my gaze to remain locked on his, not wanting to give away Cael's plan as the sphere of fire in his hands grows even larger.

"Because I—"

I don't get to finish my sentence. A ball of flame rushes toward the serpent, slamming into the back of his head in a massive explosion of fire. He cries out, relinquishing his grip on my body as he spins toward Cael.

I watch as my beloved launches several more fiery orbs, hitting the serpent square in the face. Writhing in pain it releases an inhuman screech, blasting my ears like a siren.

It twists on the floor and my eyes are instantly drawn to a deep orange glow beneath the scales of its midsection.

"Cael!" I call out, pointing to the spot.

He releases a stream of flames from his hands to that section. The serpent's scales blister and peel away from its body, revealing the meaty flesh beneath. He continues to concentrate his fire, burning a hole in its tissue until he uncovers the deep orange-red stone.

Despite the poison still coursing through me, I push myself to stand and stumble toward it. The charred and burned tissue glows red hot from the fire.

Gritting my teeth, I push my hand inside the open cavity, wrapping my palm around the magic stone. Heat sears my skin, but I force myself to hold on. This is what we came for and I will not let it go.

Reaching my hand out toward Cael, Lynx, and Astra, I call upon the magic buried deep inside me, imagining a glowing blue sphere surrounding and protecting them.

I remember now why the serpent was so hard to kill. If any part of its body is left intact, it will survive and regrow even larger than before.

Light pulses across their forms as I form the protective shield. Cael's panicked gaze meets mine.

"Kyra, no! You're too weak!"

He's right, but we don't have a choice.

"I have to burn him, Cael! I cannot let him live this time!"

Using the last of my strength, I summon the fire in my veins. Electricity arcs through my entire body. The tips of my fingers burn with crackling energy as it moves across my skin.

My every nerve lights up in anticipation as the magic forms within me, building like a giant wave behind a dam. My body trembles as I focus all my energy on harnessing my powers.

Unable to contain it, the magic bursts forth in a brilliant explosion of heat and fire, consuming everything in its wake. The serpent's body erupts into flame.

It releases a series of pain-filled cries, twisting and writhing in the fiery inferno. I grit my teeth, struggling to keep control of the protective spell that shields us from the intense heat and fire.

Cael's eyes meet mine, panic and fear flashing behind them. I stumble forward. Desperate to reach him, I drop to my knees as the flames lick at the edges of my control.

My body quakes as my strength begins to wane. "I. Can't. Hold. It."

The fire burns red hot as the structure begins to collapse all around us. The glowing blue light of the protective barrier begins the crack. Panic and fear beat at my chest as I fight to hold on, summoning every ounce of my strength to keep it intact.

I close my eyes as I focus on my powers. A warm hand alights on my shoulder. The warmth spreads from the contact and throughout my entire body, lending me strength.

I look up and see Cael standing beside me, his teal eyes locked on my own. "You can do this, my queen." He clenches his jaw and I know it is taking everything inside him to help me. "Think of home, Kyra."

An image of our castle forms in my mind. Air whips around me, and everything stills as a low buzzing hum grows louder in my ears. It quickly turns into a roaring rush of wind and then we're tumbling through a void.

Unable to stay awake any longer, I fall away into the darkness.

<h1 style="text-align:center">CHAPTER 38</h1>

CAEL

When I open my eyes, we're back in our bedroom in the palace. Lynx and Astra are still unconscious beside me but breathing. I look across the room and find Kyra lying on the floor, with an unnatural stillness that stops my heart.

I rush toward her and drop to my knees, gathering her in my arms. "Kyra?"

Panic fills me when she doesn't answer. But I breathe a heavy sigh of relief when I notice the shallow rise and fall of her chest, telling me that she still lives.

My gaze travels over her body and rests on her burned hand and forearm, the orange fire gemstone is clasped tightly in her palm. A tear slips down my cheek as I study her many injuries. Gently, I reach down and brush the hair back from her face.

"My brave and beautiful queen," I whisper. "Please, Kyra. Open your eyes, my love."

My heart clenches as her eyelids flutter and open, her face twisting in a mask of pain.

"It burns, Cael," she whimpers softly. "It hurts so bad."

A thought occurs to me, and I turn to find Astra still asleep. I gently pull her toward us, then place her on Kyra's chest, hoping and praying it works.

Sure enough the small cat disappears, fading away. I know she is joined with Kyra when her eyes glow and swirl briefly with green, then return to their normal blue. I stare down at her hand and watch in wonder as the burned tissue and the fang marks on her arm begin to heal.

"Thank god," I whisper as I lean down and press a soft kiss to her forehead.

Lynx limps up beside me and places his paw on my forearm. His eyes meet mine a moment before he disappears, and the connection is made between us. I can feel him repairing my injuries, a warm, soothing balm over my entire form as he heals me. I look down at my arm and watch as the punctured tissue from the serpent's fangs begins to close.

Kyra looks over at me, and I'm glad her features appear relaxed as Astra helps her heal. She snuggles close, then closes her eyes.

I lift her into my arms and carry her to the bed, laying her down gently beneath the blankets. Crawling under the comforter beside her, I pull her into my arms and allow myself to drift away as well.

CHAPTER 39

KYRA

A wareness slowly trickles back into my mind as I awaken. I shift slightly, and something solid and warm tightens around my waist. I look down to find Cael's strong arms around me. He pulls me back into his chest, and I snuggle against him. When I turn in his arms to face him, his teal eyes meet mine, and he gives me a sleepy smile.

"I'm glad you're awake." He tucks a stray tendril of hair behind my ear. "How do you feel?"

I test my limbs, but nothing hurts. "I feel fine. You?"

"The same," he replies.

Movement behind him catches my eye, and I laugh when I notice a pair of sharp blue eyes and a cute fluffy white face peeking over his shoulder.

"Lynx." I smile.

He dips his head in a subtle nod. "I'm glad you are both feeling well."

"Me, too," Astra adds. "You both slept for a very long

time." Her gaze shifts to the door. "You have a visitor. One of the light mages. She wishes to speak with you now that you've returned."

I look at Cael. "Tell her we will be down shortly."

Astra and Lynx go to relay our message, leaving Cael and me alone. I look at the bedside table and see the red-orange gem of the firestone on the surface next to the crown.

I meet Cael's eyes evenly. "I won't let anyone harm you."

He drops his forehead to mine and then gives me a tender kiss. "Nor I you."

I look to the foot of the bed and notice fresh, clean clothing has already been laid out for us both. I'll have to thank Lynx and Astra for this later, because it had to have been left by them.

We quickly dress and then leave to speak with the light mage. I twine my arm around Cael's. We walk down the stairs, the fire gem clasped firmly in my free hand as we approach the mage.

Anger flares through me when I realize it is Loryn—the High Mage who tried to kill Cael only a few days ago.

"Why are you here?" I ask, not bothering to hide my contempt for this woman.

"I have discovered something important, something you both must see." Her gaze goes to my hand, and her eyes widen slightly. "You found it."

"Yes."

"Word has traveled from Argeron that you destroyed the serpent trapped in the castle. Already the land begins to heal. The rains have returned, and it is believed the forest will soon overtake the desert once more."

I look at Cael, not sure how much to reveal of our missing memories, but we need answers.

"The serpent," I begin. "It mentioned something about the

request granted by the God of Creation after my death. What did he do?"

"You have not yet regained all your memories?" Her brow furrows deeply. "Even after finding the stone?"

I give her a hard look, not wanting to show any weakness.

"I still have my powers, and so does he." I look at Cael. "If you dare try to—"

"Forgive me." She lifts her hands out before her in a placating gesture. "I was wrong. I should not have tried to…" She stops, then steps forward and drops to her knees. "My queen, I thought what I was doing would protect you. It is foretold… you must be protected in this life. That is what I came to tell you. I found out what it was Bryndon asked the God of Creation for and what he was given."

"What was it then? Tell us," I demand.

"He begged the god to force you to take a harem in the next life… as you were supposed to have done in the first."

I clench my jaw. "No one will force me to do anything."

"Please," she says. "Just as your coming was foretold, this has been as well. You will take five mates in this life, and together, they will protect you."

I start to protest, but Cael steps forward.

"Where are they? How do we find them?"

My jaw drops as I look at him.

"You want me to take other lovers?" I ask incredulously.

"Of course, I don't"—he gives me a pained look—"but we do not have a choice. You need to be protected. If I made this bargain with the God of Creation in our past life, I promise you it was not done lightly. It was not done for any reason other than I love you and cannot bear the thought of losing you again."

"You should listen to him." A smile quirks the mage's lips as she stares at us. "He finally understands what must be done to protect you."

"I can protect myself," I grit through my teeth.

"Against a common enemy, yes, you can." She shakes her head. "But against a legion of dark mages and the Guardians of Destruction, you need to forge the bonds created when one takes a harem. They are soul bonds, and they are deep. Each of your mates will be able to help you wield your powers. You are stronger than any queen who has ever come before. Even now, I can feel the strength of your magic... all of us at the guild could feel it the moment you entered this world."

I think about what Nox said about creatures and people being drawn to my light. He was right.

"Your light," she continues, "is strong, and all are drawn to it, both good and evil." She pauses. "That is why the dark mages would seek to take you. They would torture you and force you to turn to their side. If that happens, all would be lost. Everything and everyone you love would be destroyed. The God of Destruction doesn't care if it all falls to chaos. That is his madness. It is the reason he must be defeated before he can disrupt the balance that has existed to keep our worlds safe from the devastation and ruin he would bring to us all.

"Because you have returned, as a show of good faith, we have already found attendants and staff eager to serve in your home. All are glad our queen has returned."

I look at Astra and Lynx, and they give me a subtle nod. I trust them to screen these people and make certain they mean us no harm. I still do not entirely trust the mages not to hurt Cael.

"How do we find the other guards?" Cael asks the mage. "The ones that will complete the queen's harem?"

I clench my jaw as anger sweeps through me. I refuse to take any other mates. I love Cael; I don't want anyone else. To take someone else to my bed would be a betrayal of my love for him. I remain silent as my dark emotions brim beneath the surface. I'll talk to him when we're alone. I will *not* be forced to take a harem.

"You will be led to them by fate." She meets my gaze evenly. "When you touch one of them, you will feel the connection at that moment, and you will know they are yours."

She tips her head to the side as she studies me. "I can see this angers you, but unfortunately, it must be done. A queen needs a harem for protection. The unbreakable bonds created between you will strengthen your powers and help you wield them." She bows low. "I will be at the guild if you need me."

When she leaves, I turn and storm up the stairs, angry at Cael for even suggesting he's okay with me taking another lover.

"Kyra, wait!"

I do not stop or turn around. I'm so angry right now, seething as I return to our bedroom. We haven't even sealed the bond between us in this life, and he's already talking about me binding myself to other men.

When I reach the bedroom, I wave my hand and slam the door shut behind me. I flex my fingers as the magic courses through my blood like fire. Willow was right—magic has its uses.

I move to the balcony and open the door, staring out at the city below and the mountains beyond that. The cool breeze whips through my hair as I consider my options. I love Cael and understand he only wants to protect me, but *I* will be the one to decide if I take another mate. I don't care what he asked of the God of Creation or what the god granted him in return. It doesn't matter. This is my life and my heart, and I will not be forced into anything.

Quiet footsteps sound behind me as Cael cautiously

approaches. I'm still angry at him, so I don't bother to turn around or even indicate I know he's there.

Tenderly, he slips his arms around me from behind and pulls me back against his chest. He presses a soft kiss to my temple and hugs me even tighter.

Despite my resolve, I melt into his embrace.

"Please, my love," he whispers against my ear. "Don't be mad at me. I only want you to be safe and protected."

Tears sting my eyes and blur my vision as I turn to face him.

"How can you ask this of me? How can you just give me away to four other men? Ask me to take them to my bed?"

His eyes are bright with tears as he clenches his jaw.

"You think I want this any more than you do?" He shakes his head as he cups my cheek. "I love you, Kyra. I can hardly bear the thought of another man touching you, but my love is stronger than the jealousy I carry in my heart. If having a harem will keep you safe… if it will keep you alive, then that is what we must do, my love."

He pulls me into his arms as hiccupping sobs rack through me, stroking his hand up and down my back in a soothing motion. I bury my face in his chest, struggling to blink back my tears.

"I don't want anyone but you. I've never even…" I stop short. "And you want me to take four lovers? Four more husbands?"

He grips my shoulders as he meets my gaze evenly.

"It is killing me to even consider it, but my nightmare, Kyra… I remember what it was to lose you. When we went to the tomb, I remembered the devastation. You don't know what I went through—the guilt, the pain, knowing it was my fault you weren't protected, knowing I'd killed you in two ways. One because I'd allowed myself to be deceived by a dark mage, and two because in my jealousy, I'd refused to share you with anyone else. You did it for me. You denied yourself the chance to form a harem because you knew I didn't want to share you."

Memories flood my mind of the first time we were together. I ran to him in the woods and asked him to take me, to seal me to him. I meet his teal eyes evenly.

"I don't want to talk about this anymore. I cannot bear it. Seal me to you, my love. I love you; I want you and only you. Make love to me, Cael."

He stares down at me with a heated gaze. "You're sure that you still want me?"

I stretch up on my toes and wrap my arms around his neck, pressing my lips softly to his as I breathe against them. "Yes."

He lifts me into his arms and carries me to the bed. Gently, he lays me beneath the comforter and then moves in beside me.

I turn to face him and he wraps his arms tightly around me, pulling me close until there is no space between us.

He dips his hand beneath the neckline of my dress and I moan as he cups my breast. "I need you," he whispers. He claims my mouth with a searing kiss as he rolls me beneath him.

I reach up and unfasten his tunic, sliding it back from his shoulders and baring him to my gaze. He groans as I run my hands over the hard planes of muscle along his abdomen and chest. I stare at him in wonder. He is masculine perfection made manifest before me.

He crushes his mouth to mine, curling his tongue around my own and deepening our kiss. I want him so much. More than I've ever wanted anything before.

He pulls at my dress, the material ripping as he tears the delicate fabric away from my body, leaving me only in my silken undergarments. He stares down at me, his gaze full of fire and hunger. "You are perfect," he whispers.

I dip my hands beneath the waistband of his pants and slide them down his hips. His length is fully erect and engorged. A bead of liquid seeps from the crown. He groans low in his throat as I reach down and gently brush my fingers over the tip.

"You are mine," he growls and then presses his lips to mine.

He kisses a heated trail down my neck to the gentle slope of one breast. He pulls the silk fabric away from my body and then closing his mouth over the already stiff peak. I breathe his name out like a sigh as he laves his tongue across the hard-beaded tip, sending small ripples of pleasure straight through me.

Heat pools in my core as fire burns through my veins. I want him more than I've ever wanted anything before in my life. He trails his lips down my stomach and then gently pushes my thighs apart. He fists the fabric of my silken panties in his hand, and I gasp as he rips them from my body. He lowers his head between my legs and then drags his tongue through my already slick folds.

A low moan escapes me as he turns his attention to the sensitive bundle of nerves at the top. He pushes one finger into my core as he teases his tongue over the softly hooded pearl of flesh, making my entire body light up with pleasure.

"Cael," I breathe. "Please," I ask, not even knowing what I'm asking for. I want everything. I want more, but at the same time, I want him inside me.

He strokes his finger in and out of my channel as pleasure coils tight, deep inside. My entire body locks up, going taut like a bowstring, then I cry out his name as I come harder than I ever have before.

I'm not even recovered from my orgasm when he moves

up my body and notches the crown of his cock at my entrance. He grips my chin, forcing my eyes to meet his. His intense gaze holds mine and the breath stutters from my lungs as he slowly enters me.

At first, everything is uncomfortable, and tight heat blooms in my core as he pushes through my barrier.

He grits his teeth. "So tight," he rasps.

After a moment, my body begins to adjust and relax around him, and when he rolls his hips against mine, everything changes from slight pain to pleasure. My mouth falls open, and a soft moan escapes me as he thrusts long and deep.

I trail my hands down his back, feeling the flex of his muscles as he thrusts up into me. The delicious friction of his cock as he strokes in and out makes my toes curl with pleasure. I'm so close to the edge. I wrap my legs around him, loving the feel of his weight over me, pinning me to the bed with each powerful movement of his body.

"Cael," I barely manage to breathe through my desire. "More."

He slants his mouth over mine in a searing kiss and moves faster.

"Tell me you are mine," he growls.

He quickens his pace as he stares down at me, his gaze fiery and possessive as his thrusts become stronger, more forceful, and deeper.

"I'm yours. Only yours, Cael."

His teal eyes stare deep into mine as he wraps his strong hand around my hip, holding me in place as he pumps into me.

I open my mouth and a low moan escapes my lips. My entire body goes tense and then I'm falling over the edge. Wave after wave of pleasure moves through me as I cry out his name.

My release triggers his own. He cries out my name as his hard length pulses deep inside me, flooding me with delicious warmth as he fills me with his seed.

Panting heavily, he collapses on top of me. I hold him close, loving the feel of him covering me completely. He carefully rolls us onto our sides, then cups my cheek, kissing me tenderly.

"I love you so much, Kyra," he breathes between kisses. "You are mine."

"Yours," I agree.

CHAPTER 40

CAEL

When we wake in the morning, Lynx and Astra greet us. I'm a little disturbed they're on the bed with us while we're still naked and wrapped up in each other, but I think I'll have to get over it. It's not as if they don't already know everything about us when they join themselves to us. They're a part of who and what we are.

Kyra turns in my arms to face them as she looks at Astra.

"What is it?"

"The royal crown," Astra says, gesturing to it on the nightstand. "You must put the fire gemstone in the setting." She lowers her eyes. "I'm sorry, Kyra, but we must begin searching for the other four guards."

Kyra jerks up in bed, pulling the sheet around her to cover her naked form.

"Why?"

Lynx steps forward, his eyes meeting mine reluctantly.

"Because we need them to help us find the other gems—water, earth, wind, and spirit."

I clench my jaw as I pull Kyra back into my arms.

"It's all right, my love. We talked about this."

"No, it's not!" Her eyes meet mine, burning with indignation. "We'll find them and ask them to help us, but I'm not taking any of them as my lovers or husbands."

"Kyra—"

"No!" she states firmly and then drops her forehead to mine. Her blue eyes stare deep into mine. "You and no other, my love."

With a heavy sigh, I nod. I'm not going to argue with her now, but I will have to find a way to convince her. She needs a harem to protect her. I will not repeat the mistakes of our past and put her in danger.

KYRA

As we stand before the mirror, the crown begins to glow even brighter. Astra touches the mirror's surface, and it begins to glow as well. Cael takes my hand, and we watch as our image ripples and distorts before showing us the interior of his apartment.

Aris walks in front of it, then stops, his eyes going wide as he stares back at us.

"Cael? Kyra?" he says, blinking in disbelief. "What are you doing in the mirror?"

A beautiful peacock moves behind him, staring at us curiously. It's long blue, gold, and green feathers spreading wide at its back in a lovely display.

"Stand back, Aris," it tells him, and I smile because I realize this is Fin, Aris's familiar that Cael told me about. "They have to come through."

His head whips back to Fin. "What are you talking about?" he asks, even as he steps away.

Together, Cael, Astra, Lynx, and I step through. Everything goes dark for a moment, then we're standing in Cael's bedroom.

Aris's jaw drops as he stares at us a moment before stepping forward and pulling Cael into a warm embrace.

"Thank god you're back! I was so worried about you, brother."

From the relief on Aris's face, it's easy to see how much he cares for Cael. Cael says they're as close as brothers, and I can only imagine how worried Aris was while we were gone.

"What happened to you?" He pulls back, then looks at me. "To both of you? When I got here, everything was a mess. I— I called the police, and they thought someone may have broken in and taken you both, and I… I didn't know what to think." He shakes his head. "I'm just so glad you're both all right."

He steps forward and pulls me into a hug as well. The moment his bare skin touches my own, warmth travels over my body, and images of my nightmare flash through my mind. I stare up at the man holding me as I lay dying, but this time, the face I see is Aris.

I inhale sharply and pull back as I meet his eyes evenly.

"It's you," I barely manage. "But how is that possible?"

He stares at me in disbelief. "You are the woman I've dreamed about all this time." His brow furrows deeply. "Who are you? And what does it mean?"

I turn back to look at Cael. "Aris," I tell him.

He nods, his gaze full of pain as he looks to the man he considers his brother. "He's one of the four, isn't he?"

"Yes."

ABOUT ARIA WINTER

Thank you so much for reading this. I hope you enjoyed this story. If you enjoyed this book, please leave a review on Amazon and/or Goodreads. I would really appreciate it. Reviews are the lifeblood of Indie Authors.

For information about upcoming releases Like me on Facebook (www.facebook.com/ariawinterauthor) or sign up for upcoming release alerts at my website:

Ariawinter.com

Want more?

Cosmic Guardian Series

Charmed by the Fox's Heart
Seduced by the Peacock's Beauty
Protected by the Spider's Web
Ensnared by the Serpent's Gaze
Forged by the Dragon's Flame

Elemental Dragon Warriors Series

Claimed by the Fire Dragon Prince
Stolen by the Wind Dragon Prince
Rescued by the Water Dragon Prince
Healed by the Earth Dragon Prince

Once Upon A Fairy Tale Romance Series

Taken by the Dragon: A Beauty and the Beast Retelling

Captivated by the Fae: A Cinderella Retelling
Rescued By The Merman: A Little Mermaid Retelling
Bound to the Elf Prince: A Snow White Retelling

Once Upon a Shifter Series

Ella and her Shifters

ABOUT JADE WALTZ

Jade Waltz lives in Illinois with her husband, two sons, and her three crazy cats. She loves knitting, playing video games, and watching Esports. Jade's passions include the arts, green tea and mints — all while writing and teaching marching band drill in the fall.

Jade has always been an avid reader of the fantasy, paranormal and sci-fi genres and wanted to create worlds she always wanted to read.

She writes character driven romances within detailed universes, where happily-ever-afters happen for those who dare love the abnormal and the unknown. Their love may not be easy—but it is well worth it in the end.

Thank you for taking the time to read my book!
Please leave a review!
Reviews are important for indie self-publishing authors and they help us grow.

Website: www.jadewaltz.com
Facebook Author Page: Jade Waltz
Facebook Group: Jade Waltz Literary Alcove
Twitter: @authorjadewaltz
Instagram: @authorjadewaltz
Email: authorjadewaltz@gmail.com
Amazon Profile: Jade Waltz

Bookbub: Jade Waltz

Project Universe Timeline:

Project: Adapt #1 – Found
Project Adapt #2 - Achieve
Project: Adapt #3 – Develop
Project: Adapt #4 - Failure

Project: F5 #1 – Bird of Prey
Project: F5 #2 – Scaled Heart

Project: Adapt #4 – Failure

Elemental Dragon Warriors:

Claimed by the Fire Dragon Prince
Stolen by the Wind Dragon Prince
Rescued by the Water Dragon Prince
Healed by the Earth Dragon Prince